Granada Hills Blood

G. Kent

Bandit Press

Copyright © 2016 by Gary R. Kent

All rights reserved. No part of this book may be used or reproduced by any means, graphic, electronic or mechanical, including photocopying, recording, taping or by any information storage retrieval system without the written permission of the publisher except in the case of brief quotations embodied in critical articles or reviews.

ISBN – 13: 978-0692599655
ISBN – 10: 0692599657
LCCN: 2015920925

Bandit Press
2329 NE 8th Place
Ocala, FL 34470
kentib@earthlink.net

This book may be ordered from the publisher, through booksellers, or online at createspace.com or amazon.com.

To E. Elizabeth Kent and the Clymer Street Gang, and all the little Vampires in Granada Hills

Contents

1. The Hour
2. Nowheresville to L. A.
3. The Routine
4. Ellison
5. Granada Hills High School
6. Ambush
7. Dr. Pares
8. The Night Hunter
9. My New So-Called Life
10. Day and Night
11. Goodbye GHHS
12. Expenses
13. Return to Dr. Pares
14. Another Friend
15. El Presidente
16. Charlie LaGamma
17. Night Prowler
18. Canyons of Granada Hills
19. The Odyssey
20. Black Bull Bowling Alley
21. Charlie the Matchmaker
22. My Vampire Girlfriend
23. A Date with Annie Mosher
24. West Hollywood Tales
25. The Return of My Maker
26. Rosamund Pares
27. Sex with Annie Mosher
28. Trouble Brewing

29. Mr. Bach?
30. Betrayal
31. Path to Destruction
32. North Hollywood
33. Killer
34. Evil
35. Annie Makes Her Play
36. Family

Graceful son of Pan! Around your forehead crowned with small flowers and berries, your eyes, precious spheres, are moving. Spotted with brownish wine lees, your cheeks grow hollow. Your fangs gleam. Your chest is like a lyre, jingling sounds circulate between your blond arms. Your heart beats in that belly where the double sex sleeps. Walk at night, gently moving that thigh, that second thigh and that left leg.

—Arthur Rimbaud

One

The Hour

It was the hour of dissolution.

I sank to the wood floor as blood seeped through the bandages on my chest. Death had arrived on the wings of betrayal. I'd been shot with a bullet dipped in mercury and, despite my most gallant efforts, the blood continued to drip on the wood floor and form a dark pool

My vampire maker had warned of such a consequence. He had predicted an early demise. My current situation appeared to validate his point.

I opened my journal and began to write.

Two

Nowheresville to L.A.

I was born and raised in Bakersfield. Not much more about that needs to be said. At Cal-State Bakersfield, I ran cross country and track with moderate success. During my time in college I had a serious girlfriend, whom I pledged to love and adore for eternity. She ripped out my heart and tossed it into an oil field. I've been floundering in the teaching profession ever since.

After college I went straight into a high school teaching job in Bakersfield. But nothing seemed to make sense. I was bogged down by a cruel and lingering melancholy. Not even Steve McQueen movies could perk me up. All my friends had drifted away after school.

My friendships have all been fleeting and transient, not always with the best results. I imagine family is the same way, but I haven't any family. There'll always be times in a guy's life when he has no friends or girlfriend. This was one of those times. During an exceptionally oppressive summer in the Field, I decided a change was necessary and moved to L.A. Well, not exactly L.A. I moved to the San Fernando Valley.

If I had to settle for the Valley, I hoped to find a place in Encino or North Hollywood, but both areas were way too expensive. Canoga Park was affordable, but Canoga Park resembled the neighborhoods of a Third World nation.

I sought advice from a real estate agent.

The lady realtor looked me up and down, and then thumbed to the financial page of my application. She said, "Canoga Park would be a perfect fit, Mr. Bach. I have several excellent units for rent in Canoga Park."

"No thank you, ma'am," I said with a wink. "I'd like to remain in the United States."

She frowned. "I live in Canoga Park."

I inquired about Granada Hills. It seemed like a favorable compromise.

"You'd have to pay a considerably higher sum than what you wrote on the application," she said. "I'd recommend against it."

"Please," I said. I was determined. "Let's take a look at Granada Hills."

She rolled her eyes. "I'll call when an appointment opens up."

I interviewed for a job at Granada Hills High School on Zelzah Avenue. Honest to God, the principal's name was Norm Mathers. His older brother was Jerry Mathers of *Leave It To Beaver* fame. I fought a mighty impulse to ask, "How's the Beaver?"

Mr. Mathers appeared excited that I had taught Advanced Placement U.S. History in Bakersfield. He said, "You look rather young to have tackled an Advanced Placement assignment."

"My pass rate was eighty percent."

He leaned back in his chair. "On the other hand, perhaps Granada is in need of some youthful exuberance."

Three

The Routine

My real estate agent reluctantly took me on a tour of Granada Hills. There were pleasant streets, like White Oak and Mission, with rows of sixty-year-old palms and eucalyptus. Most of the ranch-style homes had been built in the mid-fifties. There was a brand new Ralph's Supermarket on the corner of Chatsworth and Zelzah, and a Blockbuster's across the street.

"Seriously, Mr. Bach," the lady realtor huffed. "We're wasting our time. If you're adamantly against Canoga Park, I have some cozy units in Tarzana."

I tilted my head. "Did Edgar Rice Burroughs actually live in Tarzana?"

She rolled her eyes. "I'm sure I don't know who you're talking about."

On the corner of Chatsworth and Louise was an apartment building with a homemade sign out front advertising a two-bedroom unit.

"What about that place?"

"Oh, pooh," she said. "Those units were built during the Gold Rush."

"It looks historic."

She sighed. "In the real estate business, historic means old."

When the manager opened the front door to the available apartment, I walked across the living room to a covered balcony overlooking both streets.

"Wow," I said.

"He's from Bakersfield," the lady realtor explained.

The manager nodded.

The rooms were large, with ten-foot ceilings and vintage crown molding. There were also hardwood floors.

"I want it," I said.

After a brief conference, the realtor said, "He'll take off fifty dollars a month for one year if you do the painting."

When I offered to refinish the wood floors, the manager said he'd waive my security deposit.

"Deal," I said.

"Thank God," the realtor exhaled.

Next door to Ralph's was a Home Depot. After the Home Depot guy explained the refinishing procedure, he added, "You'll want a couple of these masks."

"What for?"

"If you get a good whiff of the fumes, you'll be high as a kite."

"Really?"

After I chose the varnish and brushes, he asked, "Don't you want the masks?"

"No thanks," I said with a wink. "I think I'll try some of those fumes."

He frowned. "Good one, smart ass."

On Saturday morning, I checked out of the Granada Inn and went to a few yard sales in search of antique furniture made from solid wood. My prize purchase was a nineteenth century oak secretary. The only new piece of furniture in the apartment was a queen-sized pillow-top bed with a wrought iron headboard.

My savings account was nearly depleted. As I waited desperately for news about the teaching job, a pleasant routine was established. I went to Ralph's for groceries, Blockbuster's for Humphrey Bogart and Steve McQueen films, and Trader Joe's for wine, coffee and other delicacies.

At night, I searched for companions at the Crying Towel Bar on Chatsworth in downtown Granada Hills. With the exception of a few drunks who mooched drinks, I had no luck. At times I missed Bakersfield and all my friends who had drifted away, but I refused to retreat.

Once a week I drove through Malibu Canyon for a day at the beach. On the south side of the Malibu tunnel I could still make out the sandblasted spot where the naked pink lady had been painted. I'd spend the day at Zuma, lying in the sun and reading Raymond Chandler novels. My favorites were *Farewell, My Lovely* and *The Big Sleep*. At times the surfers were spectacular. I watched them carve up waves off the point where Charlton Heston had discovered the Statue of Liberty in the movie *Planet of the Apes*.

Before heading home, I'd stop in Trancas for groceries and a cup of coffee at Starbucks. The Starbucks patio was situated on a wide stretch of the Pacific Coast Highway, or PCH. One afternoon, as I sipped my coffee, a mild earthquake rattled the coast and caused several patrons to scream. I found it exhilarating.

Just when the rumbling stopped, John Travolta stumbled out of the bathroom.

"Hey John," I hollered, flashing a peace sign across my eye. "What's Uma's phone number?"

He glanced at me and smiled. "Man, that earthquake scared the crap out of me."

Pulp Fiction aside, John Travolta was a funny guy.

On other days, I drove north on I-5 over Tejon Pass and hiked the trails on Mt. Pinos in the Los Padres National Forest. It was a winter recreation area, totally abandoned in the summer. On Sawmill Ridge there was a remote grove of old-growth Jeffrey pine that was an ideal spot to drink vodka tonics and search the sky for an elusive California condor. I also desired to explore the trails off the Angeles Crest Highway near Mt. Baden-Powell, but the entire area was temporarily closed due to the colossal Station Fire.

Four

Ellison

In the wine section at Ralph's Supermarket, I bumped into a sexy lady. Mid-priced chardonnay was my expertise. Watching her attempt to choose between Vendange and Sutter Home, I shook my head.

"Something wrong?" she asked.

"You can do better than that."

"I'd like to buy Kendall-Jackson, but it's so pricey."

"Overrated Napa-trash."

She giggled. "A bit of the Valley wit, I see."

I strongly recommended the moderately priced Estancia or Kenwood. "They're as good as any twenty-five dollar bottle, I guarantee."

"What are some other good brands?"

"J. Lohr and Bogle are excellent."

"I'm impressed," she said.

"Always check the alcohol percentage and make sure it's at least 13.5. Look at J. Lohr. It's 14.2."

"Why's that important?"

"Fuller body and more alcohol."

"My name is Ellison."

Ellison resembled Teri Hatcher. Not the Teri Hatcher from *Desperate Housewives*, but the Teri Hatcher in the *Seinfeld* episode who boasted, "They're real and they're spectacular."

"I'm Bach," I said, "but don't ever drink Bach wine. It's from New York."

It was amazing that the only woman I met in L.A., I found in a supermarket. Bars, beaches and Starbucks proved unsuccessful. It appeared to confirm an old urban legend that claimed the best spots to meet women were supermarkets, Laundromats and the bus depot.

Our affair lasted less than a month. The sex was not only wild, but also inspirational. Ellison was quite experienced. She had a huge mirror on her closet door, which was perfectly situated to observe our lovemaking. She enjoyed watching the clock to see how long we could last. I was like an animal.

Ellison and I went to Ralph's, Blockbuster's and Trader Joe's. We drove through Malibu Canyon to lie in the sun at Zuma and watch the surfers. I took her to Mt. Pinos to sip vodka tonics and scan the sky for a California condor. Ellison also had a desire to explore the trails off the Angeles Crest Highway near Mt. Baden-Powell, but the area was still closed due to the Station Fire.

Ellison had graduated from California State University at Northridge and was going to make a killing in the Porter Ranch real estate market. She boasted, "I manipulate both sides of the fence. I advise the seller to ask high so we have wiggle room to negotiate, and immediately inform the buyer that the seller will accept less. Of course, I keep the price right where I want it, and I don't take less than eight percent."

"Isn't that illegal?"

"I fudge the numbers well."

Unfortunately, her timing was gruesome. The housing bubble had burst and she hadn't sold a house in six months. When she discovered the circumstances of my maxed-out credit cards and unemployment, the relationship cooled and then ended abruptly.

I had told her, "I might get a job next month."

"As a high school teacher?"

"Yep. Did I tell you I know John Travolta?"

She looked me over and said, "You really are from Bakersfield."

The lack of sex didn't depress me, but I experienced difficulty with loneliness and isolation. How is it possible to feel lonely and isolated in the middle of a city with over three million people? My thoughts drifted back to Bakersfield. Perhaps it was time to lick my wounds and limp home. But in early August I got a call from Granada Hills High. My job application had been accepted.

Five

Granada Hills High School

Norm Mathers greeted me warmly. He asked me to assist with the cross country teams and I readily agreed. He introduced me to Coach Godfrey. Godfrey had twenty-seven years of experience and was strictly old school.

"Hello, Coach," I said, politely.

He stared at my longish hair and said, "You grew up in Bakersfield?"

I smiled. "Not much more about that needs to be said."

"Top dog at Cal State?"

"I won a few races. Go Roadrunners."

"You think you're a big man?"

I tilted my head. "Excuse me?"

"What's the matter, Bach? You got shit in your ears? I don't like cockiness." Mr. Mathers left the room.

"I'll store a mental note."

"Or a wise ass."

"Yes, sir."

He continued to eyeball me. "I also don't like Bakersfield. It reminds me of Texas."

"What's wrong with Texas?"

"There are only two things that come from Texas, and that's steers and queers. Which one are you?"

I shrugged. "Isn't that a line from *An Officer and a Gentleman*?"

In 2004, Granada Hills High had become a magnet for an elite academic program called International Baccalaureate. The principal and the IB coordinator were both excited about my Advanced Placement experience because they needed an American History teacher for the rising IB junior class.

The IB students were enthusiastic and brilliant. It was simple to establish positive relationships and a comfortable classroom environment. They loved to hear stories about Bakersfield.

"Tell us more about your hometown, Mr. Bach."

I said, "You know I'm from Bakersfield, you runt."

They choked with laughter.

"I spent a month one night in Bakersfield," a boy crowed.

A pretty girl added, "I'd rather live at the North Pole."

"The Valley is nice," I admitted.

"Oh, no," she said. "I hate the Valley."

"Why?"

They all chimed in.

"Too much drama."

"The Valley's an insane asylum."

"It's a smog pit."

I said, "I've noticed how small town kids yearn for the glitter of a city, and city kids want the peace of rural America. Perhaps you all would enjoy living in Bakersfield."

"Just stick a pencil in my eye," another boy said.

"Is it really that bad, Mr. Bach?"

"Coach Godfrey said it reminded him of Texas."

"What's wrong with Texas?"

In the drawl of Coach Godfrey, I said, "There are only two things that come from Texas, and that's steers and queers. Which one are you?"

The class roared.

"What did you do as a teenager?" a shy but sweet girl asked.

I sighed. "Rode my dirt bike along the aqueduct and went to beer parties in the oil fields."

The Granada Hills campus was groomed and stately. Built in 1959, the place had aged in a dignified manner. The school's nickname was the Highlanders, which had become super cool following the mega-hits *Rob Roy* and *Braveheart*. Banners proclaiming "Go Scots" were ubiquitous. In order to explain Granada's football prowess, it need only be mentioned that the field was named John Elway Stadium. The drama department boasted of alums Valerie Bertinelli, Kevin Spacey and Robert Englund, who played Freddy Kruger in *Nightmare on Elm Street*.

My classroom was bright and well-equipped. I covered every inch of wall with posters of D-Day, the Kennedy Brothers, the Vietnam War and Bob Dylan. I wowed the students with my impersonations of Captain John Smith and the Reverend Jonathon Edwards.

"You are sinners in the hands of an angry God," I bellowed. "Loathsome spiders held over the flames of everlasting hell by the grace of God; and you're getting heavy."

"Is that what you believe, Mr. Bach?"

"No, not really. It's what Jonathon Edwards believed."

"Do you believe in hell?"

I thought for a moment. "I believe hell is living your life badly."

Norm Mathers visited my classroom daily and seemed pleased. During cross country practice I ran with the boys varsity. Even Coach Godfrey started to warm up to me. One afternoon I turned on the after-burners and left the team in the dust.

One runner gasped, "I can't believe you smoked us, Coach Bach. You're a geezer."

"Careful, punk," I said. "I'm only twenty-seven. Distance runners don't reach their peak until thirty."

The J. Paul Getty Oil Company owned the foothills above the high school and granted the team permission to climb over locked gates and ignore No Trespassing signs in order to train. The acreage contained emerald slopes with seasonal creeks, sage, cottonwoods and eucalyptus.

Within a month, I officially called Granada Hills my home. I was happy and never more enthused about my profession. The faculty, however, was aloof and clannish, and didn't throw out the welcome mat to newcomers. This magnified my loneliness and isolation.

One day after school I approached two men on the IB staff and said, "Would you guys like to have a few beers tonight at the Crying Towel?"

They grinned at one another. "The Crying Towel?" one said. "That place is filled with drunks and cougars."

"It's still a bar."

The other said, "Aren't you from Bakersfield?"

My classroom was at the end of a wing right next to a covered passageway called the tunnel. From the parking lot, I walked through the tunnel past four other wings to get to my classroom. The varsity cheerleaders liked to practice in the cool shade of the tunnel.

One day I spoke to their pretty sponsor, a nice looking woman who was maybe thirty. "Shouldn't you be in uniform?"

She yawned. "I only bring out the uniform for special occasions."

"Such as?"

She thought for a moment. "Halloween might be fun."

I said, "We should go trick or treating together."

This time she smiled. "Do they celebrate Halloween in Bakersfield?"

My lone splurge after being hired was the purchase of a slightly used 2006 black Mustang. The salesman, of course, tried to cheat me.

"Don't think I can give you much for your pickup, Mr. Bach."

"It's a 4 x 4 and in damn good condition."

"It's a 1997."

I observed the manager watching us through the glass.

"Fine," I said. "Just crunch the numbers and make sure I have a low monthly payment."

He grinned. "Congratulations, Mr. Bach. You are now the proud owner of a black Mustang."

Six

Ambush

On a Thursday night I returned to Granada Hills High School to retrieve the answer notes for an essay test. When I pulled into the parking lot the campus resembled an abandoned space outpost. It was a rare evening indeed. There were no junior varsity or freshman football games, parent meetings or adult night classes. There were only a few lights and the San Susanna winds.

The school was locked up tight. I hadn't counted on that. I had no key for the gates, and the double-high chain link fence had a row of rusty barbs and razor wire on top. It was quite intimidating.

Damn it, I needed those answer notes.

How would my hero Steve McQueen get over the fence? In *The Great Escape* he would have used a motorcycle.

I wedged my toe into the first link and quickly scrambled to the top. Then I pushed down on the razor wire and swung my legs over the barbs. As I dropped to the other side, the razor wire sprang back and sliced a long gash in my forearm.

"Son of a bitch," I wailed.

A torrent of blood flowed from the wound and dripped off my fingers. Steve McQueen would not have been impressed. I tore a piece off my old CSUB t-shirt and applied pressure to the arm.

The tunnel was dark and shadowy. I walked swiftly to my room and turned on the lights. The janitors had already finished their job, and I admired the shine and luster of the room. The answer notes sat on my desk.

I turned off the lights and locked the door. Blood still seeped from the wound and I imagined I could smell it. On my way back to the fence, I entered the tunnel and noticed a tall slender figure lurking in the shadows.

"Big George?" I asked, hoping it was the head janitor. No one answered. The silhouette certainly did not resemble Big George. I stopped and squinted into the darkness.

"Hello?"

In a flash the figure pounced on me and yanked my hair. Before I could scream, fingers of steel squeezed my neck until I couldn't breathe. I swung my fists at his face with absolutely no effect. He was incredibly strong. I pried at the fingers gripping my neck, but couldn't budge them. His breath under my chin smelled of eucalyptus.

"Feisty," he said. "I like that."

Then he bit me. I thought, *holy crap, he's biting my neck!* I tried to scream, but there was no sound. I felt like I was in a Christopher Lee movie. I surrendered and the pain fled. My vision blurred and everything was warm and fuzzy. My knees buckled. He laid me down and was careful not to let my head strike the pavement.

Hot thick syrup splashed onto my lips. I began to drink. There was no taste; it was only hot and thick. I became euphoric. My veins were inflamed and energized. Then I realized the liquid pouring onto my face was blood coming from his wrist. He released my neck and stood back. I felt refreshed and spirited.

"What did you do to me, you sick jerk?"

He grinned, exposing his white fangs.

"What did you do?" I repeated.

"I'm not certain," he said, "but I think I made a vampire. I never did that before."

I rubbed my neck. "You bit me."

He said, "You drank my blood. You'll need to prepare."

"Prepare for what?"

"The thirst. It will be overwhelming."

"Oh, bullcrap," I scoffed. "There are no vampires."

"You are now a blood addict."

"I may need stitches."

He grabbed my arm. "Look, your other wound has already healed."

The gash from the razor wire was gone.

"How did that happen?" I stammered.

"Pay attention," he demanded. "Your thirst will occur at any moment."

For the first time, I took him seriously. I felt queasy. He looked like the movie star Johnny Depp, only taller and more muscular. "What exactly are we talking about?"

"You'll require a little Granada Hills blood. It will be your new drug of necessity. You don't have much time to think or plan, so listen carefully."

"I don't understand."

"Your first thirst will thrust you into an extremely vulnerable situation. It's crucial that you don't panic. I've already chosen a mark, so it will be simple and you won't attract attention. Use your new skills."

"What new skills?"

"As soon as you stand up, your new skills will become obvious."

"Who are you?"

"I've been a vampire in Granada Hills for fifty years, yet I'm still only an infant. This is the first time I've made a vampire."

"This is not happening," I moaned. "Why did you choose me?"

"I drove past the high school and saw you climbing the fence, rather clumsily I might add. I smelled the blood from your wound and decided to follow. For some odd reason, you reminded me of the movie star Steve McQueen. As I watched you in your classroom, I knew you'd be ideal. You exude a sort of melancholy I find irresistible. Life is not what you expected."

"No, it's not."

"Perhaps now you can find your way."

"I need to find an emergency room," I said.

He laughed. "Don't expect me to be your big brother. You must learn the trade on your own: it will establish your identity. After tonight you will never see me again."

"There's one bit of good news."

"A bit of the Valley wit, I see."

"My ex-girlfriend Ellison said the same thing."

He said, "You should look her up and experience her with your new vampire eyes."

"My throat is dry," I gasped. "My skin is stinging."

"I've warned you about the thirst. That's more than my maker did for me. Also, you don't need to kill them. In fifty years, I've not killed one mark. Stop drinking when they become faint. You'll sense the moment. If they die, you'll receive an incredibly pleasurable jolt. Some vampires become addicted to the jolt and turn into killers. I don't want that to happen to you."

I was trembling with pain and anxiety. "Should I be writing this down?"

"If you had not drunk my blood, you would have recovered and continued with your melancholy existence."

"You forced me."

"Not true," he insisted. "Every other mark to whom I've offered the blood has gagged and refused. You drank greedily."

My condition was desperate. "Can I bite you?"

He smiled. "You're kind of a wise ass, aren't you?"

"I still don't know what to do."

"Remember this: don't get close to them, any of them. This is crucial. They are not like us and serve only as our drug. Never, I repeat, never make friends or allow them to know where you live. If you do, you won't survive a year."

"I'm thirsty," I croaked.

"There's a pretty janitor in room D-4," he said. "Take her. Take just a little Granada Hills blood. Do not attempt to find a mark on the street."

He was talking about Janelle. She was very sexy. My face was burning up. I felt like there was broken glass in my veins.

"There must be more you can tell me."

"You're on your own, Bach."

"How do you know my name?"

He laughed. "I'm not psychic. It's on your classroom door."

"I know the pretty janitor," I said. "Her name is Janelle. I asked her for a date once, but she refused. I can't hurt her."

"If you don't kill her you won't hurt her. Just take a little Granada Hills blood and leave. She won't remember."

"Why do you keep calling it a little Granada Hills blood?"

"Granada Hills is your home territory. You won't be able to leave the town limits without feeling ill. Only blood from Granada Hills will satisfy your need."

"I can't do it."

Just like that, he was gone. The tunnel was dark and shadowy. I staggered to classroom D-4 and observed Janelle washing the smart board. She was a sweet girl. I wouldn't attack her no matter how bad I felt. She noticed me standing at the window and waved. I entered the room.

"Are you lonely tonight?" I asked.

"I like the solitude", she said. "This is my last room."

I could smell her Granada Hills blood. "Want to go to Starbucks?"

"I told you, Bach. I don't date teachers."

I shook my head. "My bad luck."

She smiled. "If I did, you'd be my first choice."

"Maybe I'll resign."

"You're pale, Bach. Are you sick?"

I left quickly. I heard a dog barking in the distance and wondered if I could chase him down.

When I reached the double-high chain link fence, with its nasty barbs and razor wire, I took one step and hopped to the other side. Steve McQueen would have applauded.

Seven

Dr. Pares

Well, this was one fine freakin' mess. I was totally ignorant about vampires. I didn't even like vampire movies. Sunrise was still several hours away. Would I burn up in the sunlight? Did I need a coffin to sleep in?

My maker was correct about one thing—the thirst was driving me insane. This must be how a strung-out heroin addict feels. I needed a little Granada Hills blood.

Then I had an idea.

From the school parking lot, I drove my black Mustang to Holy Cross Hospital on Mission and rushed into the emergency room. Hospitals had blood. I suffered from a medical condition. Maybe a doctor could help.

I informed the receptionist I was bleeding profusely from wounds to my arm and neck, and required immediate medical attention. The blood on my shirt supported my claim. She handed me a number and a dozen forms, and told me to take a seat. My number was thirty-six.

"Number nine," a voice said over the intercom.

I approached the receptionist again and said, "This will not do. I'm hurt really bad."

"Please sit down, sir," she responded. "We'll get to you soon enough."

"Ma'am," I yelped. "I'm not fooling. Look at me."

The nurse looked up and suddenly became alarmed. Perhaps it was my tone or bloodshot eyes, but she took notice and I sensed fear. She pressed a button. An intern appeared at the entrance door and motioned for me to follow. He led me upstairs to a tiny room and said, "Wait here."

I became agitated and started to scratch my chest. Sweat poured off the top of my head. I imagined headlines in the *L.A. Times*, "Gothic Horror Invades Holy Cross." Just when I decided to storm the hallway and attack a nurse, a young but haggard-looking doctor knocked on the door and entered my room. He took one look at me and slammed the door.

"Holy shit," he cried.

His nametag read Dr. S. Pares.

He held up his hand. "Stay calm. Your condition is not critical."

"I think I'm dying," I moaned.

"No, it just feels that way."

I looked at him closer. "You know what happened to me, don't you?"

He nodded. "Yes, I do."

"Can you help?"

He furrowed his brow. "Yes, but only this one time."

"My name is Bach," I said. "I was attacked at Granada Hills High School thirty minutes ago."

"I don't want to know your name. I don't want to know anything about you. I'll treat you tonight, but you must promise never to come back to Holy Cross Hospital."

"Why?

"It's dangerous. It's dangerous for both of us."

"Help me."

"Promise you won't return."

I promised. I had no choice. He left me alone in the tiny room. Perhaps he was alerting security. I walked to the window and considered leaping to the pavement. Dr. Pares returned with a plastic bag of blood.

He said, "I see the tiny scars on your neck. I know what happened and understand the power of the thirst. I worked in West Hollywood and treated many vampires in your condition."

"West Hollywood?"

"West Hollywood is vampire central."

"How many vampires are there?"

"No more questions. I'll help you tonight, but never again."

"Thank you," I said. "Thank you, Dr. Pares."

I remembered what my maker had told me about blood. "Is that Granada Hills blood?"

For the first time he smiled. "Yes," he said. "It's Granada Hills blood if it's in Granada Hills."

He set up the blood packet and slipped a needle into my arm. When the blood entered my vein, it washed away the pain. I experienced such warmth and ecstasy I didn't care if I lived or died. Dr. Pares watched me intently.

"Vampirism is full-blown addiction," he said.

"I don't care," I answered.

"Remember," he said. "You promised never to come back to Holy Cross."

"Yes, sir."

"I feel deep sympathy for you. Your strung-out feeling will return at some point every night, and there's nothing anyone can do about it."

"You're doing fine," I murmured.

I was blissfully intoxicated. Tomorrow night was light years away. I looked at Dr. Pares and asked, "How much do I owe you?"

"No charge, Mr. Bach," Dr. Pares said. "Keep your promise."

After leaving the hospital, I drove around the back streets for a few hours in order to contemplate my new predicament.

Eight

The Night Hunter

On Friday morning I called in sick to work and paced the rooms of my apartment. I kept the shades pulled down. Dr. Pares had said, "Your strung-out feeling will return at some point every night, and there's nothing anyone can do about it."

Clearly that left it up to me. But how would I approach a mark?

That evening I made my first hunting trip. I ventured out early since I had no clue when the thirst would strike. I felt normal. Perhaps Dr. Pares was mistaken about the thirst and nightly hunts, but I certainly didn't care to gamble. I assumed vampires only desired blood. Not so. As soon as the sun disappeared, I drove straight to Jack in the Box for a double cheeseburger (with Jack's secret sauce) and a chocolate shake. It tasted like haute cuisine.

After that I parked the Mustang in Ralph's parking lot and walked across

Chatsworth. My eyes began to burn. It was exactly what had happened the night before when I first experienced the thirst. It must have been my eyes that tipped off Dr. Pares. So they probably also had the potential to frighten off a mark. I sensed it was vital to stay in the shadows while hunting, just like my maker had done in the tunnel. My fangs were not out in front, like in the movies. They were further back, visible only when I lifted my upper lip. At the moment of attack, with bloodshot eyes and exposed fangs, I probably appeared quite monstrous.

Blood was like the most exquisite and delightful opiate in the world, only stronger and more alluring. In all cases of drug addiction there is a touch of melancholy and depression. To be a vampire was to suffer from the worst and most pathetic type of drug addiction on the planet.

I refused to hurt anyone. My maker had provided an excellent example. "You don't have to kill them," he advised. "They will not be harmed by losing a little Granada Hills blood." I vowed to take only small amounts and not become a fiendish killer.

My arms and chest itched. I needed some Granada Hills blood.

I hid in the bushes outside of Blockbuster's and observed the customers choosing their DVDs. Once again there was broken glass in my veins and I started to panic. In time it would become easier to control the strung-out waves of addiction, but not tonight.

I selected my mark. She appeared to stare through the glass and offer me her blood. She was in her thirties and quite attractive. She had long black bangs and shoulder-length hair. In her tight jeans and t-shirt, she resembled Jane Fonda in the movie *Klute*.

It was incredibly simple. As she unlocked her car door, I slipped up from behind and bit her on the shoulder while nudging her onto the seat. If she struggled, I didn't notice. I was very careful to take only a small amount of blood. It seemed to satisfy me. When I was finished, something totally unexpected happened. She wanted to have sex. She crawled into the backseat and pulled on my arm. Everything in my body screamed yes, but I wasn't certain if vampires were capable of having sex.

"C'mon," she urged. "I want to do it."

"I'm not sure if I can," I said, rather lamely.

"I have some Viagra," she said, sliding her hand across my Levis, "but you don't appear to need it."

I burst out laughing. "You don't understand. I'm a vampire and I don't know if vampires are supposed to have sex."

She giggled. "Let's try."

She said some dirty things into my ear while I took a little more Granada Hills blood. Then she dozed off. I watched a slender line of blood trickle down her tanned chest.

When I set her down I was careful not to let her head hit the door handle. My maker had set another fine example. I searched through her purse and found her driver's license. Her name was Hannah. I had future plans for Hannah.

Damn it! She lived in Northridge.

Nine

My New So-Called Life

Over the weekend, I tried to adapt to my new existence by watching a dozen vampire flicks from Blockbuster's. Most were ridiculous and of no help.

Bela Lugosi, John Carradine and Jack Palance showed me nothing but slicked hair, snarls and unblinking eyes. I was impressed with *The Horror of Dracula*, starring Christopher Lee and Peter Cushing, but it reminded me of a Sherlock Holmes story. Frank Langella oozed with sexuality in his 1979 *Dracula*. I watched the Langella film twice. It made me think of Hannah. *Interview with a Vampire* was ultra-cool, but Tom Cruise and Brad Pitt were too pretty and silly to be taken seriously. Brad Pitt's constant whining made *me* want to drive a stake through his heart. When I read the novel by Anne Rice, I was horrified to discover a male vampire was asexual and didn't have a penis. I pulled down my Levis several times just to make sure it wasn't true.

I couldn't fly. I couldn't turn into a bat or wolf. When I had finally come home from Holy Cross Hospital, the sun had not quite risen, but there was light. Though a pair of sunglasses would have been nice, I didn't feel any pain.

My maker had helped me more than I wished to admit. He taught me not to kill. He warned me not to get close to any human mark or let them know where I lived. Of course that didn't matter much since I didn't know anyone.

The master vampires, from Lugosi to Tom Cruise, were murderous ghouls who lived among rats and cobwebs. I slept on a luxurious queen-sized bed in a comforttable apartment at Chatsworth and Louise. There was no need for a coffin or dirt from Bakersfield. Count Dracula had been a powerful general and aristocrat with land, title and riches. I was a nobody, with little chance of keeping my meager job.

I didn't require more than two or three hours of sleep, and I never slept at night. I enjoyed food and alcohol more than ever. In fact alcohol seemed to ease the pangs of withdrawal and arouse my sexual desire. My robust sex drive was a pleasant discovery. Not only did I not lose my penis, I believe Anne Rice would have been rather impressed with its new size and shape. I constantly preened in front of the mirror and studied my new cat-like appearance. I had pale skin with large dark eyes. How could all the books and movies be so wrong? It was obvious no vampire had ever written a book.

One stereotype that was deadly correct was the one about needing blood every night. I was a hopeless blood addict. Also, whenever I fumbled my way outside of the Granada Hills city limits, I became painfully ill. That had to mean my maker hunted in the same neighborhoods, though I never saw him. We both lived on Granada Hills blood.

My maker had also warned me about other vampires who were vicious killers, addicted to the jolt of death. The thought made me nauseous. I believed I felt that way because my maker wasn't a killer. I learned how to leave tiny fang marks behind the neck or shoulder that would be inconspicuous and heal quickly.

On Saturday, I watched college football on TV, while nibbling microwave popcorn. I especially enjoyed watching the UCLA Bruins. But I was still lonely and isolated. I wasn't certain why my maker abandoned me, but I supposed he had good reason.

Ten

Day and Night

I needed to go to work, but work was a day job and day had the sting of the sun. Since nearly every other myth about vampires was incorrect, perhaps the day and night thing was also wrong, or at least exaggerated. Obviously I hadn't died on my way home from Holy Cross Hospital in the early light.

My attack had occurred on Thursday night. On Friday, I called in sick and had my date with Hannah. I didn't feel the need to go out Saturday night, so maybe Dr. Pares was wrong about the nightly blood fixes.

Early Sunday morning, I ventured outside of the apartment. The weak rays of the sun touched my cheek. My face burst into flames and ...I'm kidding!

Nothing much happened. It stung a little, but was tolerable. I went back inside and put on my CSUB hoodie and sunglasses. I decided gloves would attract too much attention, so I kept my hands inside my pockets. I strolled the neighborhood from Louise to White Oak and didn't feel too uncomfortable. My skin continued to prickle and I sweated profusely. The brightness seemed to cause the most unpleasantness. My eyes watered and blinked.

Inside my apartment, I donned a gray long-sleeved Under Armour shirt and stood at the window. I had no reaction. The apartment could remain bright and cheery during the daylight hours. One of the best vampire films I had rented was *Near Dark*, starring Lance Henriksen and Jenny Wright. It was about a coven of vampires who prowled the countryside in a Winnebago with tin foil covering the windows. The film was funny and quirky, but also incorrect. Still, perhaps I would tint the windows of my black Mustang for comfort.

Unfortunately, my days of sunshine at Zuma Beach and Mt. Pinos were over. Even if I went at night, both areas were well outside the city limits of Granada Hills. Guess I'd never get a chance to climb Mt. Baden-Powell.

Since I perspired so much in the daytime, I decided to joke with my students that I suffered from hot flashes at age twenty-seven. Though my classroom had excellent air conditioning, I bought a box fan for extra cooling power. I assumed most vampires chose not to go out during the day, and that was probably how the myth had begun.

My appearance continued to alter. I grew paler. Though I ate heartily, I became thinner and even taller. My face was gaunt, with high cheekbones, heroin chic, I joked. After all, I was an addict. It also appeared I wore heavy mascara like a stage actor or rock star. These changes were more noticeable during the day. At night it was much easier to blend into a crowd. I was strong and swift with natural grace. When stalking a mark, I could dash up from behind and nip their neck without using my hands. The mark would never even see my face.

My new obsession was cleanliness. I showered and shampooed every few hours, and brushed my fangs constantly. My teeth appeared whitened. I sprayed my body with *Dark Temptations* by Axe or Calvin Klein's *Escape*. My attire consisted mostly of jeans, Nike cross-trainers, and a black t-shirt over a long-sleeved Under Armour shirt. I called it my Brad Pitt outfit—from his movie *The Mexican*. Julia Roberts had also starred in that movie. She would certainly be a nice lady to look up, though I seriously doubted she spent much time shopping in Granada Hills.

My prize accessories were a delicate gold choker chain and a cross. It was comforting to believe Jesus still loved me. After all, I wasn't a killer.

The extreme addiction depressed me and tugged at my soul. Whenever the need for a little Granada Hills blood heightened, I became panic-stricken and irrational. A strung-out vampire is a menace to society and himself. There had to be a way to keep it balanced.

My other major downer was loneliness. I felt even lonelier now because there seemed virtually no chance for camaraderie. My maker insisted I not get close to humans. He claimed they were not like us and served only as our drug. If I told them where I lived I'd face annihilation.

Early Sunday evening I strolled out of Blockbuster's with an armful of old westerns, including *Pat Garrett and Billy the Kid* with James Coburn and Kris Kristofferson. As I passed a car with its window open, a female voice said, "I know what you are."

I stopped and looked inside the car. In the passenger seat was a sexy redhead wearing athletic shorts and a black sports bra. It was a good hunch her boyfriend was inside picking out a movie.

I said, "How do you know?"

"I just do."

I slipped into the backseat, and then tugged her over the console and plopped her on my lap. "What do you know, little red?"

"I've seen other vampires," she announced proudly. "I used to live in West Hollywood."

"Does your boyfriend know that?"

"He's real lame."

When I bit her she pleaded with me to help take off her shorts. I looked inside the store. "We don't have time."

"Yes, we do," she insisted. "My boyfriend becomes mesmerized when he's inside Blockbuster's."

"Okay," I said. I did want to try it. I slid off her shorts and tossed them into the front seat. She lifted her knees and arched her back. Each time I bit her, she performed a move out of the *Kama Sutra*, or so I imagined.

Eleven

Goodbye GHHS

Things appeared to be normal at Granada Hills High School. I returned to work on Monday and remained indoors. My International Baccalaureate students were incredible. For some reason I felt sharper and more focused.

For our IB Internal Assessment grade, we decided to do a group performance. It would be filmed and the process documented, and we would use the entire IB junior class as actors, directors, producers, writers, stagehands, set builders, camera and lighting operators, costume and make-up artists, and technical advisors. The performance was to be a commentary/comedy on women's rights.

Using the personal correspondence of John and Abigail Adams, we staged a saucy exchange between the two on the eve of John heading off to help write the Declaration of Independence.

In the bedroom, Abigail proclaimed, "When you and your gentlemen friends are declaring independence from tyranny, do not neglect the ladies."

John quickly responded, "We know better than to give up our husbandry rights within the legal system."

"You may change your tone when the ladies withhold certain husbandry rights within the bedroom," Abigail shot back.

The kids roared with delight.

In the final scene we linked the famous couple with Lucretia Mott and Elizabeth Cady Stanton at the 1848 Seneca Falls Convention. In ghostly form Abigail appeared on the scene pulling John by the ear and inspiring the ladies to foment a women's revolution.

"All men *and* women are created equal," thundered Elizabeth Cady Stanton.

The kids laughed their asses off. They loved the ghostly appearances and sexual hijinks. When I predicted high scores, Norm Mathers and the IB coordinator were very pleased.

I was also a big hit on the cross country team. In my hat, sunglasses, Under Armour shirt and sweat pants, my job was to discuss strategy and explain the daily workouts at our team meetings under the bleachers of John Elway Stadium. My insight and desire had completely won over Coach Godfrey. He admired my philosophy of mental toughness and praised my contributions to our early victories.

However, I did begin to notice subtle changes on campus. Members of the faculty often gave me double takes. Students blatantly commented on my appearance and obvious physical changes.

"Mr. Bach, are you wearing make-up?"

I invented an explanation. "I've earned a role in UCLA's production of *Dangerous Liaisons.* The goop from rehearsals is hell to wash off."

The gorgeous cheerleading sponsor began to act wanton. She offered to accompany me to the Crying Towel Bar in her cheerleading outfit. Her aggressive behavior confounded me. Even Janelle, the sexy janitor, came to my room and asked if I was coming back in the evening to fetch an answer key.

I sensed trouble.

When two senior girls remained after school and began to act overtly seductive, I lied about a new career opportunity and resigned. It broke my heart, and also compounded my sense of loneliness and isolation.

Twelve

Expenses

After quitting Granada Hills High School, my finances plummeted to a precariously low level.

Well, it takes a thief, Mr. Grant.

I found it lucrative to target affluent-looking marks like well-dressed gentlemen or high-maintenance ladies. After drinking a little Granada Hills blood, it was simple to snatch their valuables. I usually took only money, but if expensive pieces of jewelry were in plain sight, I swiped them too. I believed it wise to build up an ample supply of gold and diamonds, for emergencies or in case I needed a quick escape.

Sometimes I reached out and grabbed a purse or billfold so swiftly the mark never realized it had been pinched. In stores and restaurants I'd slip my hand into a register and palm a wad of bills. No one ever noticed. Often my take was over two hundred dollars. I then took my act to banks. John Dillinger, America's most notorious bank robber, once said, "Go to where the money is." My first haul netted two thousand dollars.

I rented a safe deposit box at Security Pacific next door to Ralph's. Most of my money and all the jewelry were placed inside the box. I never stole from Security Pacific. That would be like pissing in the tent. I hid money all over the apartment, in desk drawers, books and coat pockets.

It was fun to invade the big department stores at night and steal clothes, DVDs, CDs and even furniture. I chose only the most expensive items. I broke into Ralph's and walked out with a box of porterhouse steaks and a case of La Crema chardonnay. I crept into the REI store and took state-of-the-art backpacking equipment in case I needed to flee. Plus, I loved to play on the rock-climbing wall.

Though I hadn't gotten sick, I still thought it wise to maintain a family physician, so I decided on a second visit to Dr. Pares.

Thirteen

Return to Dr. Pares

I required serious advice. Only two people in the universe knew I was a vampire and one of them had vowed never to see me again. That left Dr. Pares, and he needed to step up to the plate. I drove to Holy Cross Hospital in the early evening hoping to escape the usual lunacy that occurred in the ER after midnight. Fat chance. The place was bedlam.

I hung around the waiting room for about fifteen minutes. When a small boy with a broken arm was admitted, I latched onto his party and pretended I was a family member. I continued down the hallway alone, and no one challenged me—not at first.

After I searched several rooms, hoping to find Dr. Pares, a stern-looking Nurse Ratched blocked my path and said, "Sir, privacy laws prohibit you from entering other patients' rooms. Which room is your party?"

When she blinked her eyes, I darted up from behind and blew a kiss on her neck. She wheeled around and saw me inches from her face. I hissed and bared my fangs, causing her to swoon and fall into the arms of Dr. Pares.

"You!" he cried. "You could have given her a heart attack. What are you doing here?"

"We need to talk."

"No, we don't. You gave me your word you wouldn't return to Holy Cross."

"That was an unfair promise," I said, "and you know it."

He looked at me and said, "Are you wearing make-up?"

"Sure," I said with a wink. "I bought it at House of Ghouls on Balboa."

For the first time, he smiled. "You look more like a rock star."

I gave him a once over. "And you look like Dr. House."

An orderly stood in a doorway. "Shall I call security, Dr. Pares?"

At that moment a pretty little girl raced down the hallway and promptly slipped on the freshly waxed floor. She would have suffered a nasty spill if I hadn't zipped to the spot and caught her with one hand.

"Careful, darling," I said.

The little girl ran to Dr. Pares. He handed her over to the orderly and said, "This man is my patient, thank you." He led me to an empty room.

"Thanks for seeing me," I said.

He nodded. "You helped my daughter."

"She seemed to be someone special."

"I've never known a vampire to perform a good deed."

"You're my doctor," I said. "There's no one else I can trust. I'm looking for answers."

"I don't know what I can offer."

"You've known other vampires," I said. "Tell me about them."

He sat down in a chair and motioned for me to join him. "None of the other vampires were like you. In West Hollywood the vampires are vicious murderers. They threatened my family for blood and morphine."

"I would never harm you or your family. You're my only friend."

"I was forced to leave West Hollywood before I lost my license or they killed me."

I tried to test him. "Couldn't they just follow you to Granada Hills?"

"I don't think so," he said. "Vampires are very territorial about their blood. That particular bunch would never leave West Hollywood."

"They may not be able to leave," I informed him. "My maker said I would become ill if I tried to leave Granada Hills."

He was quiet for a moment. "I didn't know that, but it makes perfect sense."

"Why did they demand morphine?"

"It's a cheap blood. In high doses, morphine produces a similar sensation to blood. They demanded large quantities, and became violent if I refused."

"I pose no danger to you or your family. I'm not a killer."

"I wish you no harm, Bach," he said, "but you need to understand that I know how to deal with vampires."

I lifted my eyes. "You do?"

"In West Hollywood, I inadvertently discovered a way to protect myself."

"How?"

He said, "I attempted to take a vampire's temperature."

He brandished a thermometer and walked toward me. At first I was bemused. Then I blanched and retreated to a corner. I felt weak and nauseous.

"What is it?"

"Mercury."

"You took my temperature two weeks ago."

"I used a digital device."

"Back up," I gasped, "or I'm going to faint."

"Mercury is deadly poison to a vampire," he said. "If I hold it close or splash it on you, your powers will diminish and you'll become vulnerable. If I poured it on a knife or needle and broke your skin, the wound would never heal or stop bleeding. Never. You might survive a small cut with gauze and tape, but a deep gash would eventually kill you. The pain would be unbearable and you'd wish for death. Bullets dipped in mercury are especially nasty and lethal."

"Does anything counter the effect?"

He hesitated. "I don't know. I've been searching and experimenting. I once kept a vampire alive for six weeks who had a gunshot wound to her chest."

I tilted my head. "Why did you bother to help?"

"I'm a doctor," he said, "and she had never threatened me. Since vampires exist, I feel the need to help if they are sick or hurt. Also, the ability to heal or fend off a vampire might come in handy one day."

I smiled. "You've taught me a few lessons tonight. Please let me visit occasionally. Perhaps one day I can help you."

"Why would you help me?"

"I want to be friends, Dr. Pares. I'm lonely, and the addiction to blood is depressing. Don't turn me away. I'll be a loyal friend. Remember, I didn't choose to become a vampire. I was victimized."

Dr. Pares fell silent. Finally, he said, "Thank you for aiding my daughter. You do seem to be a different breed of vampire."

"Be my friend?"

He hesitated. "I hope I won't regret it."

"I may be able to do you a favor one day," I said. "All you need to do is ask."

We shook hands. "Consider us friends, Bach."

"Good," I said with a wink. "May I try a little morphine?"

Fourteen

Another Friend

As I hurried across the busy hospital parking lot, there was a spring to my step and my spirits had definitely been lifted. I wasn't alone in the world any longer. Dr. Pares was my new friend and I was certain I could count on him in a pinch.

I noticed the tall skinny man leaning against a slick BMW long before he noticed me. He was smoking a cigarette. Though the morphine was doing its trick, I briefly considered taking a little Granada Hills blood. But since my spirits were soaring I ignored the opportunity.

The guy turned his head and said, "Bach? Is that you?"

I halted. It was startling to hear my name pronounced by a stranger. I stared at him.

"Do I know you?" I asked.

"Bach, it's Charlie LaGamma. Cal State Bakersfield cross country, dude. Go Roadrunners."

It seemed I had forgotten everything associated with Bakersfield. Well, almost everything. I still pined for Annie Mosher, even though she had unceremoniously dumped me.

At first I didn't recognize Charlie LaGamma. Then I burst out laughing. Charlie and I had been teammates on the first Bakersfield State cross country team to win the region and qualify for nationals. We took sixth place in the NCAA Division II at St. Cloud, Minnesota. Charlie looked similar to Matt Damon in *Good Will Hunting.* You'd think I'd know him anywhere, as they say, but his presence was so out of place in Granada Hills that it took me a minute.

I said, "Dude, what are you doing here?" On the Bakersfield State qualifying team, everyone was known as "dude." We were all cult followers of Jeff Bridges in *The Big Lebowski.*

He walked up to me. "I was visiting a friend."

"No, I mean, what are you doing in Granada Hills?"

"Damn, Bach. No one wants to spend their entire life in the Field."

We shook hands and hugged.

He examined me closely. "What the hell, dude? Are you wearing make-up? I feel like I'm in a scene from *The Phantom of the Opera*."

"Funny," I said. "You're a real funny guy. I have a role in *Dangerous Liaisons* at UCLA."

"Still the stage actor, eh?"

"What about you, dude? What have you been doing?"

"I'm a crooked broker," he said with a straight face. "Let's have a drink and catch up."

"I'm not keeping you from anything?"

He shrugged. "*Nada, amigo.*"

"Where do you want to go?"

"How about Donte's on Laurel Canyon?"

That was no good, I thought. Donte's was in Studio City. "Let's keep it in Granada Hills."

"Okay," he said. "El Presidente on Sepulveda and Rinaldi serves a killer margarita."

"Excellent." A little tequila with the morphine might be good enough for tonight.

"Follow me, dude," he said, walking back to his BMW.

I watched him unlock his car door. Holy crap! Two friends in one night. I said, "It's swell bumping into you, Charlie. Go Roadrunners."

"Right back at you, Bach," he said.

Fifteen

El Presidente

On the corner of Sepulveda and Rinaldi was a sweet traditional Mexican restaurant with a covered patio bar called El Presidente. It had the best handmade margaritas in the Valley. The night air had cooled down and it was starting to rain. Several groups of loud drinkers were whooping it up on the patio while enjoying a playful Santa Susanna breeze.

Charlie LaGamma found a table near the bar and waved to a chunky barmaid in a tight red mini-skirt. Charlie and I had a positive history. Not only were we teammates on a national-qualifying Division II cross country team, but we also ran the 5,000 meters in track. I hadn't seen him in five years.

At El Presidente, Charlie and I picked up where we had left off, and hit our stride on the second margarita. Our choice was the Cadillac margarita with pure lime juice, Gran Patron Silver, and no ice. When the tequila began to deliver its kick, we ordered *huevos rancheros* with the fried eggs over hard.

The elderly waiter frowned. He looked like a slimier version of John Astin from *The Addams Family*. "Over hard?" he said. "Seriously?"

"That's right, dude," Charlie said. "Not runny."

"Suit yourself."

The jukebox was playing some kind of urban rap that was profane and irritating. I decided to put on some alternative tunes. As I stood in front of the jukebox, scanning the selections for Green Day or U2, a trio of bandana-clad Chicanos surrounded me.

The first one said, "Don't mess with the tunes, Anglo."

"It's my turn," I answered.

"Did you take a number? If not, you don't have a turn."

"I already put in a five-dollar bill."

"Say *adios* to your five bucks."

The second one stepped up closer to examine my face. "How come you all dolled up, *chica*?"

I looked at him. "Excuse me?"

"Are you wearing eye make-up?"

"Nope."

He grinned at his friends. "This Anglo *es muy bonita, verdad?*" The others snorted with laughter.

"You can have two of my picks," I offered.

"I already told you, you don't have a turn."

I tapped B-9. "You'll like this song."

He pinned me against the jukebox and snarled, "You stupid *puta.*"

I said, "Be cool, *amigo.*"

He became enraged and snatched me by the hair. "Don't patronize my heritage, Anglo. You aren't part of *La Raza.*"

The trio was about to roughly remove me from the vicinity of the jukebox, and I was going to let them, when suddenly Charlie LaGamma dashed to my rescue.

"Let him go, *Zapata,*" he said, grappling with the third one.

I was touched by his loyalty. Unfortunately, like most tall, skinny, former long distance runners, Charlie was no Sugar Ray Leonard. He was quickly collared and knocked to the ground.

Without thinking, I reacted. In one swift motion I seized the offender with one hand and hurled him across the entire length of the patio, over the adobe wall and into the parking lot. The other patrons let out a collective gasp.

To the one who had pulled my hair, I said, "Okay, dude, you can pick out the songs. Have a closer look."

I grabbed him by the neck and smashed his face into the jukebox. Turning to the last dude, who was by now trembling with fear, I bared my fangs and hissed loudly. He bolted for an exit.

The covered patio bar at El Presidente fell deathly silent. "It's a Beautiful Day" by U2 began to play on the jukebox.

Charlie LaGamma sat sprawled on the tiled floor.

"Go Roadrunners," I said meekly.

He looked up and said, "Dude, we need to talk."

Sixteen

Charlie LaGamma

When Charlie LaGamma plopped down on the leather couch in my apartment, I spilled the beans. I told him the story of my attack and how I had been looking for blood at Holy Cross Hospital. I did exactly what my maker had advised not to do. Charlie listened intently. In fact he perked up when I explained how I made my living.

I also told him about my addiction to Granada Hills blood.

"So you can only drink blood from people who live in Granada Hills?"

"No," I explained, "I can only drink blood from people who are inside the city limits of Granada Hills."

He said, "I feel like I'm in a Christopher Lee movie."

"Don't say that, dude."

"Why not?"

"Christopher Lee always died in his films."

Charlie then proceeded to ask all the normal dumbass questions.

No, Charlie, crosses and wooden stakes don't do the trick. At least I was wise enough not to mention Dr. Pares or his discovery about mercury.

No, Charlie, I can't turn into a bat or wolf.

He got all jazzed up when I related my cravings for food, drink and sex.

Afterward I felt like I had gone to confession. It was a relief to come clean and share my story. Charlie LaGamma was keenly interested and sympathetic about my plight. I couldn't understand why my maker had warned me to stay away from friends.

Charlie told me about his job. "It's a company called Whittaker and Bean, dude. I'd like you to come see my luxury townhouse in North Hollywood."

"I'd like that, dude, except..." I explained the home turf rule. "I get weak and sick outside the city limits. I could die."

"Bummer, dude."

Charlie did have some unfortunate news. Like many brilliant stockbrokers, Charlie suffered from bad judgment when it came to his own finances. He had invested heavily in real estate just before the market crashed. I almost asked him if he knew Ellison. He had shifted his focus to high-risk ventures, and finally became addicted to online Texas Hold'em. He was in a bad fix and asked if I would consider taking him along on a few burglaries.

"Let me be your partner," he said. "I could drive and be a lookout."

"Maybe we can go out this weekend."

He hung his head. "I'm really ashamed, dude. I need money just to get through the month."

"Come with me Saturday, dude," I said. "I'll give you the entire take."

"I'll pay you back, Bach."

"Shut up," I said. "You insult me. Whatever I give you is not a loan, it's a gift."

His eyes glistened and he teared up. "I won't forget it, dude. You and I have always been tight. Remember how we pushed each other in the 5,000?"

"I remember," I said. "Those were the best years of my life."

He smiled. "I remember letting you beat me quite a bit."

"The money means nothing to me, dude."

"I still want to pay you back. I have something better than cash."

I was intrigued. "Like what?"

"Information, dude."

"What information?"

"I'll bet you remember Annie Mosher."

Her name was like a slap in the face. Annie Mosher was the girl who had stomped on my heart at Cal State Bakersfield.

"Yep, I remember her."

"She lives right here in the Valley, dude. I know where she works."

"Sure you do."

"It's no mystery. I'll prove it."

Seventeen

Night Prowler

I discovered the decadent pleasure of roaming the alleys at night. Granada Hills was filthy with alleys. In 1958 the Marlboro Construction Company built their final tract of four hundred homes on the old John Carroll ranch and installed a system of alleys so homeowners wouldn't have to pull into or out of heavy traffic. Most were dimly lit by 1930s-style lampposts and lined with towering black poles connected by heavy electrical wires. Garage doors and fences of wood or block, many covered with ivy, shaped the borders.

It was fascinating to peer over fences and spy on the lovely people. Most were hunkered down, but some sat at computers while others worked on projects in their garages. Sometimes I would observe a small intimate gathering or late barbeque. There certainly seemed to be more arguing and fighting going on than lovemaking.

Teens often hunkered in the backyards, gulping down their parents' alcohol or pharmaceuticals and smoking weed.

My favorite alley was off Chatsworth and Hayvenhurst. Water ran down its center and drained into Bull Creek wash. The washes in the San Fernando Valley were notoriously raucous territories. East Valley gangs staged rumbles, while mobs of teenagers held parties under the bridges with an anything goes mentality. There was usually a smorgasbord of drugs and alcohol along with plenty of sex and brawling. Even the legendary Los Angeles Police Department practiced a system of containment rather than bother with the hassle of breaking them up.

I was never tempted to explore a wash, but the alleys possessed a special allure. During my nightly wanderings, dogs never barked at me. At one time, in the recent past, dogs had been predators and perhaps they recognized a brother-in-arms. I was always respectful of dogs and cats, and sometimes we even nodded to each other. It was extremely rare to bump into people in an alley...until tonight.

Two teen couples stumbled carelessly down the center of the alley behind

Kingsbury. They were heavily sedated and boasted loudly of their exploits at a party on Clymer Street, laughing about the enormous amounts of drugs and alcohol they had ingested.

One of the girls sang a line from Pink Floyd. "I-I-I-I-I-I have become . . . comfortably numb."

"You're wasted, babe," her boyfriend croaked.

"We're all wasted," the other girl said.

"Who has the sloe gin?"

The boyfriend said, "Wait until we get to my backyard."

I sank into the shadows and observed.

Three of the teens failed to notice me, but the last girl looked in my direction and smiled. When she attempted to speak, she slurred her words.

"Hel – lo, you wanna par-tay?" she said.

I clamped onto her wrist and pulled her into the shadows. When I bit her neck she moaned huskily. The others stopped to watch. At first no one spoke. Finally, her boyfriend discovered his tongue.

"Who the hell is that?"

He marched toward me with clenched fists. I seized hold of his neck with my other hand and bit him, too. For a moment I alternated sips. The girl stumbled back against a garage door and rolled her eyes. Two thin lines of blood streamed down her white tank top.

The second male, realizing something was horribly wrong, lunged at me with a blade. I propped his friend up against a fence and leaped to the roof of the garage. The boy stood in the center of the alley swinging his knife into the air. I pounced on him and took a little more Granada Hills blood. When he went limp I carefully set him on his back, making certain his head didn't bang on the asphalt.

The second girl shrieked and fled into the darkness. I chased her down quickly. When my fangs were firmly planted in her shoulder she calmed down and became sensual.

"That feels so good," she murmured.

This one was a looker. When I stopped drinking, she said, "Do me more."

"What do you want?" I asked.

"Do me," she whispered. "Do me good."

I was slightly taken aback. "I don't think so, darling."

"Do me standing up." She lifted her tight mini-skirt and wrapped a long leg around my thigh. It was tempting, but she couldn't have been older than seventeen. Where had she acquired such experience?

"You're sweet," I said, setting her down on her pretty ass. "I may be a vampire, but I still have scruples."

She giggled.

I left them all weak, but very much alive.

Eighteen

Canyons of Granada Hills

Although the alleys had grabbed my attention, voyeurism being a curious trait of the vampire, it was the canyons in the north foothills of Granada Hills that captured my imagination. The rugged hills had dozens of sharply cut canyons; some were located on the privately owned J. Paul Getty property, while most were part of the North Valley Conservation Preserve.

Though the sun was only a minor inconvenience, I still preferred to visit after dark. The night offered peace and tranquility, with the opportunity to commune with nature and the local wildlife.

Wiley, Bee and Towsley Canyons were excellent examples of the local terrain when the huge Spanish *haciendas* dominated the Valley, but my favorite spot to visit was Rice Canyon. It was a natural playground with tall grass, cottonwoods and eucalyptus. A year round creek ran boldly down its center. The preserve trail ended in a box canyon that was topped with big-cone Douglas fir. Rice Canyon was also the best place to encounter animals. The coyote and mountain lion were my brothers. I was able to communicate with them by using my eyes. We appeared to possess a mutual respect and understanding, and it was a tender bond.

I never desired to kill a human being, but I would kill anyone who harmed the animals. One day I might be forced to retreat into the canyons and join them. Prey animals like deer instinctively fled from me, but I would never hurt any of them either.

One night in the empty unlit parking lot, I surprised a ranger who was placing a ticket on the windshield of my Mustang.

"Good evening, Mr. Ranger," I said loudly. "Something wrong?"

He leaped into the air. "Jesus, sir," he answered. "You didn't have to sneak up on me. You failed to pay the three dollar parking fee."

"I wasn't aware."

"There's a sign at the gate."

"It was dark when I arrived," I explained.

"Sorry about that."

"Can I pay the three dollars now?"

He said, "Too late, sir. I already wrote the ticket."

"What's the fine?"

"Seventy-five dollars."

I whistled. "Pretty steep."

"Sorry, again."

"Can I purchase an annual pass?"

"You'll have to come by the station."

"I have an idea," I said. I pulled out my wallet and counted ten new one hundred dollar bills. "Will you tear up the ticket and call us even?"

He stared at the pile of Ben Franklins. "What are you doing out here so late, sir?"

I shrugged. "It's the best time to converse with the coyotes."

"Fine," he said. "You don't have to tell me."

I grinned. "I dislike crowds."

He looked me over with his flashlight. "Are you wearing make-up?"

"Maybe."

He pocketed the money. "Park here anytime, sir."

Nineteen

The Odyssey

It was a wet and foggy night. Charlie LaGamma and I were taking the long uphill drive to the Odyssey Restaurant. We planned to discuss business.

The Odyssey was the finest and most elegant restaurant in Granada Hills. It was perched high on a hill above Rinaldi, the last major boulevard before the foothills. President Bill Clinton had dined here while touring the damage from the 1994 earthquake. Beyond the Odyssey were the canyons of the North Valley Conservation Preserve. From its windows or large open patio the views of the San Fernando Valley were stunning, even on a wet and foggy night.

Charlie LaGamma said, "I appreciate a couple hundred bucks, Bach, but I need more. A lot more."

"I can get you more."

"I want to be fair, dude. I want to do my part."

A pretty hostess opened the front door. As we entered the restaurant, Charlie said, "Quick, gimme a fifty."

I did. A well-heeled crowd surrounded the reservation desk.

"Do you have reservations, sir?" another hostess asked.

"Nope," Charlie answered.

"It will be about an hour wait."

Deftly flashing the fifty-dollar bill, Charlie said, "Do you have a patio table next to a fire?"

The hostess smiled. "Follow me, gentlemen."

Charlie and I were seated next to a fire pit with a soft gas flame. One and a half million lights flickered in the Valley. The light fog blurred the streetlights on Rinaldi. Our meal was exquisite and we shared an excellent bottle of Anderson Valley chardonnay. We talked mostly about Bakersfield.

Our waitress had obviously been informed of our tip to the hostess and hovered over us like a jealous girlfriend.

Charlie laughed. "We're going to have to give her a hundred bucks."

I shrugged. "I'll swipe it back at the register."

"I like it when you talk that way, dude."

As we sipped our wine I noticed a slender girl with jet-black hair sitting at the bar. Several men stopped for a word. She was a cool customer, neither obliging nor cruel. She dismissed each offer with a smile that contained perfect white teeth. I got the feeling she was on the prowl for someone special. Then an elderly gentleman walked past her and I saw her snatch his billfold. No one else saw her do it. I was surprised, not by the theft, but by her deft sleight-of-hand. She was a vampire. Her high cheekbones and heavy make-up, or what appeared to be make-up, reminded me of myself. She was an odd beauty. Her pale arms and legs were highlighted by a seductive black dress hiked up to her mid-thigh. As I watched her, not once did she appear to notice me.

"Things were going strong in 2004-05," Charlie lamented. "I took the money home in a wheelbarrow. Then clients started to take a bath and the market crashed. I ran up huge debt. North Hollywood is an expensive neighborhood."

"You could move to Granada Hills."

"That wouldn't help much."

I turned my full attention to him. "How much do you need, dude?"

"A lot."

I poured another glass of wine. "It won't be a problem."

"I don't ask for something for nothing, dude" he said. "I can be of service to you. I can run errands during the day and leave Granada Hills. I also have something real sweet to offer."

"What kind of a deal are we talking about?"

"Money is simple for you, dude. Next time you have an opportunity, grab me a handful. What I have to trade is well worth it."

"Let's get outa here," I said, handing our waitress two one hundred dollar bills.

On the way out we passed the register. Five or six servers were trying to cash out. In a swift motion I reached between the servers and snatched a handful of bills. Even Charlie didn't catch my move. In the parking lot I handed him the entire haul. It was over fifteen hundred dollars. He let out a gasp.

"Sweet, dude."

"I don't want anything in return," I said. "You're my friend and I can get you more."

"I'm no leech, Bach," he said. "I have a surprise for you."

"What's that?"

"Remember who we talked about the other night? A special girl? You're going to be blown away, dude."

We drove down the hill from the Odyssey and made a left on Rinaldi. At Sepulveda we turned south and passed El Presidente and Hamer Ford, the monstrosity of a dealership where I had purchased my black Mustang.

Charlie said, "Turn right on Mission. At Woodly take a quick right and pull over."

I parked beside La Rosa Liquors and turned off the engine.

I said, "Okay, what?"

He pointed. "Look across the street, dude. Do you see it?"

I glanced around. "No."

"Check out the bus benches."

I looked. Initially, I didn't comprehend. Then I looked closer and saw the advertisement on the second bench. It read, "Annie Mosher of Remax Realty," and had a picture of Annie, my old

Bakersfield flame, navigating a Remax hot air balloon.

I shook my head. "Son of a gun. Another real estate agent."

Charlie asked, "What do you think about a partnership?"

"Do you know where Annie lives?"

"No, but I will. I have a contact at Remax who will access her personal file, for a fee."

"Get it done, Charlie," I said. "I'll pay well for the information."

"Consider it done, dude." We bumped fists. "I want to do my part. It makes me feel like I'm earning my cut. My debts are dragging me down, and it can really wear on a guy's sexual energy.

We parked in the back of my apartment building. Charlie said, "I really do like your neighborhood, Bach. Maybe I will move to the Hills."

"There are two apartments available in the building."

Charlie drove off to North Hollywood in his BMW, and I took a long walk. As I strolled under the misty streetlights and eucalyptus trees that lined White Oak, I thought about how I had broken nearly all the rules. My maker said to never let anyone get close. I screwed that one up with Charlie and Dr. Pares. Don't allow them to know where you live. Now Charlie wanted to move into the building. With a little luck, I planned to smash more rules with Annie Mosher. My maker would be astonished. Well, so what? He wasn't much of a pal. He did tell me one bit of truth. He said, "You'll never see me again." So far he had kept his word. I certainly didn't owe him any allegiance. Yet the more I examined our short time together, I began to realize how much he had tried to teach me. I assumed he knew best. How else had he survived fifty years? I had barely survived fifty days.

I just hated to be alone. My maker insisted a vampire had no use for friends, but I needed contact. I hated loneliness and isolation.

Twenty

Black Bull Bowling Alley

The following evening I returned to the Odyssey in search of the slender vampire girl. When I described her to the hostess, she said, "If I saw a girl matching that description, I'd race to the door screaming." Then she winked at me and said, "Or maybe I'd run to you for protection."

I almost got sidetracked. "Perhaps we could look for her together."

"I get off at 2:00 a.m."

I stored a mental note. The vampire girl was not inside the restaurant, so I went out to the fire pits. There were several lively groups of professional ladies who were quite tempting, but I really wanted to find the black-haired vampire beauty.

It was soothing to stand next to a fire pit and feel the chilly Santa Susanna wind swoop down from Mission Peak. After sipping a glass of Jameson's on the rocks, I paid up and sat in the Mustang until midnight. I never saw her.

I drove to the Black Bull Bowling Alley on Sepulveda north of Devonshire. It had become one of my favorite haunts. Though I didn't bowl, I enjoyed the atmosphere. I had recently discovered the joy of prowling on rooftops, especially the big department stores like Lowe's, Target and Costco. Most, however, had alarms that had to be dealt with. When I crept across the roof of the Black Bull, I found an unlocked trapdoor and climbed down to the bar.

At the bar I encountered a pleasant surprise.

Back in the summer of 2002, a group of college friends and I drove to Las Vegas for a weekend of reckless gambling, drinking and whatever. We never got there. The moment we crossed the state line we stopped at a dilapidated gas station/bar that advertised slots and poker. My friends were ecstatic. I wasn't foolish enough to sit at one of the poker tables and be plundered by the semi-pros wearing cowboy hats and sunglasses, so I settled in front of a slot machine with fifty dollars worth of tokens. Then I noticed the chalkboard.

It read, "Falstaff Longneck and a shot of Fleischmann's – $2.00."

Holy crap! I loved Falstaff, but it was almost impossible to buy in Bakersfield.

I said to the barmaid, "Keep 'em coming until my friends lose all their money."

"You seem like a fun date," she said.

The Black Bull Bowling Alley carried Falstaff draft. It was possibly the only bar in the Valley to have it on tap.

After I took my first sip I heard a commotion on the roof. Company was arriving. I melted into the shadows and waited. Four gang members from Pacoima, with spiked hair and leather coats, slipped through the trap door and jumped to the floor. After some initial horseplay they marched to the bar and attacked the stock of the finest whiskeys. I watched them from the corner. As the whiskey began to weave its magic, the boys whooped it up and played with their switchblades. When I finished my draft I strolled between them to the bar.

"Pardon me, dudes," I said, "but you're making far too much noise. You could attract Five-O."

The punks were incredulous.

"If you drink too much of the expensive stuff," I added, "the owner will become suspicious and surely discover the unlocked trapdoor. Then none of us will drink for free."

"How'd you know about the trapdoor?" the leader growled.

"I like to play on rooftops."

"Get lost," he demanded. "I mean it. I'm gonna count to three."

"I was here first," I replied.

They looked at one another, and then back to me. The leader grinned. "What's your name, smart ass?"

I stepped into the soft light. "My name is Bach."

They burst out laughing.

"Back off, girlie boy," a second one hissed, "or I'll cut you."

"Let's have a drink together," I suggested, and reached for the Maker's Mark.

"I'll cut you," he threatened, raising his blade.

I paused. "If you swing that blade at me, I'll bite all four of you."

He hesitated. "What did you say?"

The third one said, "Leave him alone. Let's all have a drink."

The biggest one stared at me. "Why are you wearing make-up, dude? Are you a transvestite?"

"I'm an actor."

They laughed even louder, and with more enthusiasm.

"You want to drink with us, girlie dude?" the second one asked.

"Sure."

He handed me a bottle. "Drink up, and then I'll cut you good." He brandished his switchblade in front of my nose.

"Thanks," I said, taking a full swig of Maker's Mark.

"Let me kick his ass," the big one said.

I looked around the bar. "Perhaps if you clean up your mess, no one will notice our little intrusion."

The leader said, "I'm appointing you our maid."

The big one stood up from his stool and stripped off his shirt. "I'm going to teach him some manners."

"Leave him alone," the third one repeated.

"Shut up. I wanna hurt him."

The leader tossed a full glass of Maker's Mark in my face. "There you go," he said. "Help wash off the mascara."

The shirtless one said, "This is gonna be fun."

I held up my hand. "Dude, chill out."

"You're a comedian with make-up. That makes you a clown."

"Just beat the shit out of him," the leader demanded.

The shirtless one threw a vicious haymaker punch. I caught him under his arm and hurled him through the front tinted window. Shattered glass rained into the parking lot and an alarm went off.

"Sadly," I said, "the owner is sure to notice that."

The others froze. I seized the leader, who was now yelping and sniveling, and dragged him to the nearest bowling lane. With perfect form I rolled him down the alley and he smashed face first into the pins.

"Strike," I snarled, and bared my fangs.

"Mother of God," the second one shrieked. He dropped his knife and tried to climb to the trapdoor.

I pulled him down by the leather coat and bit his neck. Blood poured off my chin. When I was finished I placed him on the floor, making certain his head didn't strike the tile.

The third one shuddered. "Please," he said, "don't kill me."

I pulled him to the bar. "You stuck up for me, dude. Let's have a drink. Make it quick, however. Your buddies may need an ambulance."

Police sirens howled on Sepulveda.

"Let me give you some advice," I said. "Next time you run into a guy who looks like he's wearing make-up, don't mess with him. He could be a vampire."

Twenty-One

Charlie the Matchmaker

Charlie LaGamma arrived at my apartment with Annie Mosher's address and phone number.

He said, "She lives in Chatsworth near Del Vista Ranch."

"Where'd you get these pictures?"

"Off the Remax Website. There's a ton of them."

I handed him eight thousand dollars.

"Sweet, Bach," he choked. "You're the dude."

"*No problemo.*"

"I called and told her about you."

I stiffened. "That may have been a mistake. I'm not sure how I want this to play out."

"No, it's cool. She's excited and wants you to call. I was only trying to help, dude."

I put my hand on his shoulder and dropped another seven thousand dollars into his lap. He sat on my leather couch and stared at the money. Tears streamed down his cheeks.

"Don't do that, dude," I said.

"I can't help it," he blubbered.

"You've earned it."

"This money will really help," he said. "You may be a vampire, but you're still my best friend."

When he left I called Annie Mosher. It rang several times before she answered. I immediately recognized her husky Lauren Bacall voice.

"I've missed you, Bach," she said. She actually sounded sincere. "But please, no pressure. I'm don't know if we should see each other."

I said, "Let me buy you a drink at the Odyssey in Granada Hills. If you feel comfortable, we'll have dinner."

I could hear her breathing. "It may be our only meeting. Do you understand?"

"Yes." I dreamed of a reconciliation, but wasn't sure how I really felt. I also doubted she'd be ecstatic about dating a vampire.

I said, "I'll meet you in the parking lot. I drive a black Mustang."

She giggled. "I hope I recognize you. Charlie said you look different."

I sighed. "I've been doing some stage work at UCLA. My hair is longer and I'm a tad thinner."

"Do you wear make-up?"

I chuckled. "That bastard LaGamma. What else did he tell you?"

"Only that you wear heavy eye make-up and are kinda pretty."

"It's for the play," I lied. "I'm playing an eighteenth century aristocrat in *Dangerous Liaisons*. The eyeliner is a bitch to wash off."

"I'm teasing," she said. "You were always quite grand on the stage, and I'd recognize you no matter what role you're playing."

That could be a challenge. I wondered if I should tell her I'm playing a vampire in the next production. I loved the scene in *Interview with a Vampire* where Antonio Banderas was on stage playing a vampire pretending to be a vampire.

I said, "Nice picture of you in the balloon on the bus bench."

"Smart ass," she scolded. "Maybe I won't meet you."

"Drinks and dinner at the Odyssey, Annie," I said. "After that we never have to see each other again."

She said, "I'll be looking for a pretty eighteenth century aristocrat in a black Mustang at nine p.m."

Following our conversation, I couldn't decide whether I should be happy or wary. I still had powerful feelings for Annie Mosher, and suspected she was well aware of that fact. With any luck her pictures on the Remax Website were all photoshopped and she had gained two hundred pounds.

Yeah, fat chance!

Twenty-Two

My Vampire Girlfriend

The trailhead to Rice Canyon was two miles past O'Melveny Park on Old San Fernando Road. The canyon seemed a million miles from Los Angeles. In the late afternoon the waist high yellow grass glistened in the sun as tiny aphids flitted in the cool air. Early evening brought in a heavy mist.

The trail ended at the top of a hill studded with several large black oaks. As I approached the hill, hoping to hook up with a coyote, I spotted a girl standing perfectly still in the mist next to the largest oak. A backpacker, I thought, but as I got closer I didn't see a tent or any other equipment. She stood with her back to me.

I slipped into the shadow of the creek so the bubbling water would muffle my footsteps. I employed extra stealth and precaution. When I was certain I was directly below her I got on all fours and scaled the bank.

She was crouched on the edge of the rim waiting for me.

"Not very Apache," she said. "I heard you coming from the tall grass."

"Impossible."

"Actually, you were quite clumsy."

I said, "I couldn't hear myself over the rushing water."

"I heard you." She proceeded to describe my exact route up the trail, including the precise spot where I dropped into the creek bed.

"How did you do that?" I asked, eyeing the back of her neck.

"Don't you think about biting me," she scolded. "I'm one too."

I held back. "One what?"

She bared her fangs. "You know, snarl bite suck."

It was the pretty vampire girl. I hadn't recognized her in the dark. She was wearing tight jeans, hiking boots and a black leather jacket. Her jet-black hair was braided into two ponytails. She barely looked twenty-one years old.

"You're the girl from the Odyssey."

"I saw you scoping me out at the bar," she said.

"I didn't think you noticed. You're the first vampire I've ever seen."

Her eyes widened. "Didn't you see your maker?"

I nodded. "I saw him, but it wasn't much of an occasion."

"You've been looking for me?"

"Sure," I said. "I wanted to introduce myself. You're a vampire and a very lovely lady."

She leaned in closer to my face. "Do you want to have sex?"

I choked and coughed. "Do vampires have sex with one another?"

She burst out laughing. "You don't get out much, do you?"

"I'm young and don't know much."

She smiled. "Sex among vampires is not a wise decision because it can lead to complications. But we can still do it."

"What complications?"

"It might create attachments. We may start to care about one another, and that can be dangerous. It's best to have sex only with the marks."

"I don't understand," I said. "What's wrong with caring?"

She said, "Didn't your maker explain this to you?"

I shook my head. "He didn't explain much."

"Attachments lead to destruction."

"Don't you ever get lonely?"

"Never."

"I'm lonely all the time," I said.

"It'll pass."

"How long have you been a vampire?"

"Twenty-seven years and twelve days. You?"

"Seven weeks and three days."

She told me she lived in West Hollywood and only came to Granada Hills to prowl the Odyssey. Her story sounded dubious. She also claimed she knew I was a vampire the moment she saw me dining with Charlie LaGamma.

"You shouldn't mix with them socially," she commented.

I shrugged. "What attracted you to this canyon?"

"You," she said. "I followed you here, and then raced up ahead."

"How are you able to leave West Hollywood? I get sick when I step outside Granada Hills."

"You're not in Granada Hills now."

"Yes, I am. Old San Fernando Road is the northern boundary to Santa Clarita."

"Do you want to have sex?" she repeated.

I grinned. "I thought you were kidding."

"Nothing kinky. Just normal sex with a little bite."

"Bite?"

"You'll love it," she assured me. She smelled like sage. "But we can only do it once. No attachments."

I looked her over. She was serious. "Fine by me."

"Good," she said. "Take off your clothes."

Twenty-Three

A Date with Annie Mosher

Annie Mosher was not very impressed. She looked me over and said, "Your hair is too long and you're too skinny. You also look taller, if that's possible."

"I've had a few tough weeks."

"Charlie said you quit your job."

I hung my head. "That's true."

"Are you looking for a new one?"

"Well..." This was rapidly turning into a train wreck. Annie had matured beautifully and grown even more attractive, and she knew it.

She sighed and bowed her head. "I've no business talking about careers. My real estate job crashed with the market."

"Perk up," I said. "Maybe I'll buy a condo."

She smiled. "You need money to buy a condo, smart ass."

"I know how to get money."

"Good. I don't have to worry about paying for dinner."

I stared at her. "You look amazing. I didn't think it was possible for you to get prettier."

"You're sweet, Bach." She peered at my eyes. "You are wearing eye make-up. Don't deny it."

"I told you," I said. "I have a role in *Dangerous Liaisons* in a UCLA production. The damn goop is impossible to wash off. We open in two weeks. Would you like to be my special guest on opening night?"

I was bluffing, of course, but I suspected she knew it. No telling how much Charlie LaGamma had told her. She was a different woman, more confident and much more provocative. Verbally sparring with her was a new treat.

The Odyssey Restaurant began to work its spell. We had a small table on the patio with the San Fernando Valley at our feet. She actually attempted to apologize for the wretched way she had treated me in Bakersfield, but I waved her off. No need to open old wounds. I wanted desperately to bite her shoulder and have long luxurious sex, but Annie was not a mark. I didn't want to sound too eager.

She surprised me when she said, "I'd love to see your apartment. Charlie said it's historic and shabby chic."

"It does have a certain dilapidated elegance," I joked. "Come over for drinks and dinner next week."

"What's wrong with tonight?"

Now she sounded too eager. I don't know why, but I hesitated.

"I want us to go slowly," I said. When she began to pout, I added, "I also want the place to look its best."

Then she set a powerful lure. "I want to spend the night with you at your apartment, Bach."

A red flag should have popped up, but I wanted her so badly and didn't care. "Meet me next Saturday in the Odyssey parking lot."

"Don't you want to pick me up in Chatsworth?"

"I can't leave Granada Hills."

"Why not?"

"I'll explain next week."

I knew if we had sex I'd tell her everything. My maker would probably drive a stake through my heart if he knew what I was planning. I had to have her. She was never much impressed with my acting or running, perhaps my vampirism would win her over.

"You look sexy," she conceded. "Almost pretty."

"Thanks, I think."

It took all my will power not to drag her out to the Mustang and ravage her in the back seat. She kissed me softly on the lips.

"Next week," she whispered.

Twenty-Four

West Hollywood Tales

I began a nightly haunt of the Odyssey Restaurant. I had many more questions for the slender vampire girl. My method was to sit in the cavernous parking lot while listening to the rock band U2. I liked their songs "Vertigo" and "In The Name of Love." Or I found a place at the bar and ordered the most expensive sipping whiskey.

One evening I asked the bartender, "Have you seen a slender girl with shiny black hair, pale skin and wearing a tight mini-skirt?"

He thought for a moment. "Does she look like an extra from a vampire movie?"

"That's her."

"Not tonight," he said, "but when she's here she's usually not alone."

I nodded. "She knows how to attract a crowd."

He grinned. "What about you, dude? Are you wearing eye make-up?"

"Funny," I said. "I never heard that one before. The girl and I are in a stage production. We come here after rehearsals and are still in make-up."

Four nights without luck. I assumed she was serious when she said we'd meet only once, but she favored the Odyssey and I was betting on a return.

On the fifth night I decided to have dinner.

The hostess said, "It'll be about a thirty minute wait."

"I'll be on the patio."

"Yes, sir," she said, staring a little too long at my eyes.

I brought my drink to a fire pit. The misty view of the Valley was magnificent. The slender vampire girl was sitting alone at a table and staring at the car lights on the 405.

I sat down next to her. "I want to know how you're able to leave West Hollywood."

She didn't look at me. "Figure it out yourself."

"Tell me about life in the Hollywood hills."

She appeared to anticipate the question. "West Hollywood is a vampire mecca. My apartment building has twelve units and vampires occupy nine. We joke it's a vampire *Melrose Place*. No one bothers the other three units."

"Do you know your maker? Does he live in the building?"

"He's gone. He made every vampire in the building, and then left. He is very old, perhaps five hundred years. He never spoke to me after our special night. I feel safe in West Hollywood. I have no relationships with the other vampires, but there's an unwritten code that we would unite in the face of a common threat."

"Why can't I leave Granada Hills?"

She rolled her eyes. "You can," she said. "Just like venturing into the sunlight, you can adapt to different situations. It's difficult, at first. Dracula himself moved to London with a coffin filled with his native dirt."

"Dracula is such a lame story."

She snickered. "Some believe Bram Stoker was a vampire who purposely invented the silly myths for protection."

"Why can't I recognize other vampires?"

"You're too young. Your eyes haven't developed. No doubt you have been very near other vampires, and they knew you.

Until you are able to recognize them, you are in the utmost danger."

"Why?"

"Killer vampires do not tolerate non-killers," she said. "They aspire to annihilate us."

"You're not a killer?"

"Of course not. Otherwise, you'd be dead."

"Why did my maker abandon me?"

"I'm sure he watches over you all the time."

"Then where is he?"

She winked. "He's around."

I looked her over. She reminded me of a young and very sexy Winona Ryder. Her breath smelled of sage. "I'm glad I met you."

There was a hint of a smile. "Go back to Rice Canyon in one hour. This must be our last time. Neither one of us can afford to care about the other."

Twenty-Five

The Return of My Maker

When I returned to my apartment he was sitting on the leather couch with a full glass of my finest chardonnay and watching a recorded episode of the reality series *Survivor.*

He said, "This is a fascinating show. Eighteen people try to outwit, outplay and outlast one another. At the end of each show, someone is voted off the island in a tribal council. Do you like it?"

"Not particularly."

"That's because you'd be the first contestant voted off the show."

"Why do you say that?"

He stood up and roughly pushed me into a chair. "You know very well, Bach. You've screwed up. I'm here to save you."

"I didn't think I'd ever see you again."

"You're not supposed to see me. That doesn't mean I don't see you. My maker watched over me for thirty-four years until he got careless and was destroyed. He checked on me every night, and I saw him twice."

"How was he destroyed?"

"It wasn't the humans," he said. "A gang of killer vampires caught him in a deadly trap."

"I'm doing okay."

"No, you've been reckless. You'll be lucky to last out the month."

"I'm still alive."

"Two simple rules. Number one, don't let them get close. You can't have human friends. They'll never like or trust you, and they'll only want things from you. Charlie LaGamma only wants money."

"Annie doesn't want anything."

"Please," he said. "Annie Mosher wants to become a vampire."

"How do you know?"

"I know her type of female mark, and they all want to be vampires."

"She doesn't even know I'm a vampire."

He frowned. "Charlie told her."

"She's not a mark."

"Oh, I forgot," he said. "You love her."

"Yeah, I do."

"She knows that, Bach. She's manipulating you."

It did seem plausible. Annie appeared quite anxious to come to my apartment. I said, "So what? I don't care. Charlie is my friend, and I want to get back with Annie."

"You're a fool."

I sighed. "I'll be more careful."

"Number two, don't let them know where you live. Charlie already knows, and you plan to bring Annie here in two days. Which parts of the word "don't" do you misunderstand? You should move out of here immediately and break all contact with them both. Then there's Dr. Pares. Beware. He has experience with vampires."

I hung my head. "What do you care?"

"It's simple, Bach. I watch over you. We're family."

I looked up. "Why didn't you tell me this before?" I wailed. "Why can't we spend time together? I'm not like you. I need friends. I can't handle the loneliness and isolation."

"Give it time," he said. "Most vampires are destroyed in their first year because of mistakes. You've made plenty. If you can just last for one year, you will learn most of what you need to survive. Each succeeding year you'll increase your chances of reaching the century mark. In a year or two we can have more contact. But right now it's too dangerous. Bad luck can strike at any time. My maker was over eight hundred years old when he was struck down by dumb bad luck. If you want a girlfriend, you should stick with the tall slender one."

I shook my head. "She said we couldn't be together."

"She's playing hard to get, Bach. She may be a vampire, but she's still a female. You don't know much about females, do you?"

I thought for a moment. "Nope."

"If we let our guard down, a human can outsmart us. You must move from your apartment tonight. I'll help you. Do not, let me repeat, do not meet Annie Mosher in two days."

I looked him over. He really did look like Johnny Depp with height and muscles. "Thanks for your concern, but I can't make any promises. I love her."

He said, "I should kill them both. I'd be doing you a favor."

I smiled. "Annie and Charlie are safe with you. You're not a killer."

He nodded. "Neither are you. Killing robs you of your soul."

"I don't even know your name," I said. "What is it?"

He pushed a lock of hair out of his eyes. "You're joking. You don't recognize me?"

For a moment I was confused. Then it hit me. "Holy crap! You really are Johnny Depp."

He held up his hands. "Well, I ain't Edward Scissorhands."

Twenty-Six

Rosamund Pares

Dr. Pares glanced up from his desk and took off his glasses. "I've been expecting you, Bach," he said. "I'm glad you're here."

I feigned surprise. "Really? I thought you said it was too dangerous."

"It is too dangerous, but I wanted to see you."

"What for?"

He paused. "We may be able to help each other."

"You've been very kind," I said, "and I need all the kindness I can get."

He looked me over. "You appear healthy. Is something wrong?"

I sat down and blurted it out about Charlie and Annie. "I've been very stupid. My maker gave me two rules and I broke them both in two weeks. I'm breaking the rules by visiting you. I just can't handle being alone."

"I understand."

"I need to learn how to protect myself from myself."

He shook his head. "Mercury is your worst nightmare. Any human who has knowledge of mercury can destroy a vampire. Mercury smeared on any sharp object is a lethal weapon. If your skin is pierced you will bleed to death."

"I met a vampire from West Hollywood. I wonder if you know her." I described the tall slender black-haired girl.

"I've only met two females, and one died. Most of the vampires from West Hollywood are vicious killers. How is she able to leave West Hollywood?"

"I'm not sure, but this one is not a killer."

"I certainly wouldn't have forgotten the one you describe."

"There must be others who know about vampires and mercury. Don't you think there are vampire experts and maybe even hunters?"

"I'm sure there are."

"I still don't understand why you experiment with mercury," I said. "You already know it can kill."

"I want to discover a cure. I believe I'm very close."

I was still confused. "You want to save vampires exposed to mercury?"

"Not all vampires," he said, "but I'd save you."

"Why would you save me?"

He said, "If you know I'd help you, perhaps you'd help me."

"Of course I'd help you." What was he up to?

"Follow me."

He led me up the stairs and down a long corridor with a low ceiling. We entered the last room on the left and he locked the door. On a bed was an elegant looking woman who was obviously dying. She looked at me and smiled. I felt instant melancholy.

Dr. Pares took me into a corner and said, "This is my wife, Bach. Her tumor is inoperable and incurable."

I continued to stare at the woman. "I'm sorry. My mother died from a tumor."

"I like you, Bach," Dr. Pares said. "You appear genuine and sincere. I feel the same way about loneliness. When she is gone, I fear I'll no longer care to live. What will become of my daughter?

"I wish I could help."

"You can help, Bach, and I'd be in your debt."

I glanced up. "Excuse me?"

"I promise to do anything for you at anytime."

"I don't understand."

"Help her."

I shook my head. "I don't know what I can do."

He took hold of my arm. "Make her a vampire."

I was aghast. "What?"

"Please," he begged. "If you make her a vampire, she might not die from the tumor."

"I – I can't do it."

"Also, I need a sample of your blood for my experiments," he said. "The more I learn about mercury, the closer I am to potentially saving you."

"Dr. Pares, I don't know how to make a vampire."

"Nonsense. Someone made you. How did he do it?"

I thought back to that night in the tunnel at Granada Hills High School. "I don't remember. He bit me and everything went blank. You saw me within the hour."

He asked, "If you bite someone and they don't die, do they become a vampire?"

"Of course not," I answered. "I bite someone nearly every night and no one has turned into a vampire."

"Then there has to be something more. Think, Bach. What else do you remember?"

I gripped my throat. "The blood. I remember the blood. I had blood in my mouth and I drank it."

"Where did the blood come from?"

I finally remembered. "It was him. My maker had cut his wrist and offered me his blood."

"You drank his blood?" Dr. Pares said. "That must be it."

"I felt electrified and wanted more. He attempted to set up my first mark, but I knew her and couldn't do it. Instead, I came to you."

"Then the movies are wrong. You don't become a vampire by being bitten. You must drink a vampire's blood."

"That seems correct," I said.

"Then do my wife."

I shook my head. "Dr. Pares, it may not work. She could die."

"She's dying anyway, Bach. No medical procedure can save her."

"I'm frightened. I've never done it before."

"Please," he begged. "I'm willing to suffer the consequences."

"I'm not a killer."

"I won't let her bleed to death," he said. "No matter the outcome, you can always count on me for anything."

"I – I..."

"Do it, Bach."

Though her face was ashen, Dr. Pares' wife was still very pretty. "Okay, I'll try," I said, "but I'm only eight weeks old."

"Do your best."

"You must prepare for her thirst."

"How?"

"Blood, of course. If I'm successful, you must quickly inject her with blood."

"I'll get the bags," he said.

When he left I locked the door and held my breath. Then I charged her with my fangs exposed and bit her on the neck. She stiffened and grabbed the bed railing, but I held on tightly until her grip weakened. She moaned softly.

I found a scalpel on a table and cut my wrist. I let my blood splash on her mouth. Initially she wouldn't take it, but when the blood touched her tongue she drank until

I withdrew my arm. I felt weak. I wasn't sure what would happen next.

Dr. Pares pounded on the door. I waited. When I finally let him in, his wife was sitting upright and alert. Her eyes were shining. I was exhausted.

I said, "I believe it worked, Dr. Pares. You are now married to a vampire."

He embraced his wife and kissed her face. She responded with bursts of laughter. "I don't feel the pain anymore," she said.

"Bach," Dr. Pares stammered. "I..."

"Don't thank me yet," I warned. "We still don't know how this will turn out. I'm supposed to watch over her, but I don't know what to do."

He introduced us. "This is Rosamund, Bach. You needn't worry, I'll take care of her."

Rosamund took my hand and kissed it.

"Give her the needle, doc," I said.

He glanced at me. "Whatever you need, whenever you need it."

Twenty-Seven

Sex with Annie Mosher

When I confessed to Annie Mosher about my vampirism she became giddy with a hint of hysteria. We were sitting inside my Mustang in the Odyssey parking lot. She immediately asked all the dopey questions I expected. The fact that she was aware of my circumstances created an endangerment I found intoxicating. She gazed at me with her huge green eyes in a new and seductive manner.

"I'm telling you all this to give you a chance to escape."

"You don't scare me," she said. "I wear a cross."

"So do I." I held it between my fingers.

"Yipes," she cried. "I guess I'm doomed. Do you sleep in a coffin? That might be a real turn-on."

"Forget the movies, Annie," I said. "I sleep on a Sealy pillow-top bed and I'm a clean freak."

"Charlie claims he met you during the daytime."

"The sun is only a minor inconvenience. If I cover up and wear sunglasses, I can venture out."

"What about mirrors?"

"Please."

"I know I'm sounding lame, Bach," she said, "but I don't meet a vampire every day."

I said, "I'm still learning. I'm only nine weeks old."

"Are you invulnerable?"

She may have caught my hesitation. "I suppose a falling meteor would do the trick."

"Silver bullet?"

"Annie, I'm not a werewolf."

"Do you know any werewolves?"

"I don't believe they exist."

"What about drinking blood?"

"Sadly, that is true," I said. "Blood is the drug of necessity for a vampire. However, I've never killed anybody. Vampires don't have to kill. I take only small amounts of blood, and leave them very much alive."

"Do they turn into vampires?"

"Stop it. I need a drink."

"Of blood? Are you going to bite me?"

"Of whiskey, silly." I flashed my fangs and she jerked back.

"Jesus," she yelped.

"Let's talk about you," I said. "Tell me more about your life."

She ignored the question. "Can you make a vampire?"

She appeared way too eager. Perhaps Johnny Depp was correct.

"No, I can't," I lied. "It's a complex process and only the older vampires can perform the procedure. Maybe one day I'll learn."

"Can you have sex?"

"Why not?"

"Vampires in the Anne Rice novels lack—the tools."

"I don't believe Anne Rice is a vampire."

"So sex is no problem?"

"Better than ever." I took hold of her arm and she didn't resist. "I like to combine sex with a little Granada Hills blood."

"Granada Hills blood?"

"Granada Hills is the place of my birth. I can only drink blood that is physically in Granada Hills. Also, I can't leave Granada Hills. If I do I become ill and could die."

"Please don't think me slutty, Bach," she said, "but all this talk about blood and sex is turning me on. It's not like we haven't done it before."

On the short drive to my apartment we didn't speak. The balcony doors to the bedroom were open. Annie moaned in her husky Lauren Bacall voice. Her fingers wound tightly behind my neck and she wrapped her legs around my hips.

Her seduction was premeditated. She wasn't wearing a bra or panties. I should have been more suspicious, but like I told Johnny Depp, I didn't care.

My girlfriend was back.

Twenty-Eight

Trouble Brewing

Charlie LaGamma's role in my reconnection with Annie Mosher compelled me to be extra nice to him. Perhaps I tried too hard.

"I promise to help, dude," I said. "I owe it to you."

"Is it going well with Annie?"

"Better than before."

"Good for you, Bach."

We watched the cars on Chatsworth from the balcony of my apartment. "I do worry about consequences," I said.

"What consequences?"

"I'm not sure. Every time something good happens there are consequences. Sometimes the consequences don't make the good worth it."

Charlie tilted his head. "That's deep, dude. Maybe without the consequences nothing good would ever happen."

I nodded. "You may have a point."

"C'mon, dude," he said. "Don't be so serious. It'll drag you down. When did you start believing in karma?"

"I'm a vampire now," I said. "What are the consequences? Am I in league with the devil?"

"Don't be ghoulish, Bach. There is no devil. Vampirism has its advantages."

"Such as?"

"Money," he said, and frowned. "Money is no longer a concern."

I was more than a little surprised. I had given Charlie over thirty thousand dollars in two weeks. "Is money still a concern for you, dude?"

"I've got major cash problems. I'm a fool for women and they take advantage of it."

"Join the club of everybody."

"I also have gambling debts. Some bad people are after me."

"I can protect you."

"No, you can't. These dudes are too good and too many."

I said, "Okay, dude. Tell me what you need."

"I need a really big score," he said. "I'm no mooch, dude. I gave you Annie gift-wrapped."

Two days later, we parked beside a Wells Fargo armored truck in front of Ralph's Supermarket and, in a matter of seconds, I made off with fifty-two thousand dollars. I gave it all to Charlie. We celebrated at El Presidente with *huevos rancheros* and Cadillac margaritas.

"Drink up, dude," I said. "Enjoy yourself."

"I'm still down, Bach."

"What are you talking about?"

"To climb out of my mess, I'm going to need triple this take."

"Holy crap. You are down in a hole."

"I've been burned by risky investments. I have to park my BMW on the next block to keep it from being repossessed." His voice began to rise. "What's the big deal, dude? You can get more money."

I shook my head. "It might be dangerous if we move too quickly. The Wells Fargo heist is going to attract some heat. Someone could identify us."

He snapped his fingers. "Let's drive to San Diego for a big score."

"I already told you, dude. I can't leave Granada Hills."

"Because of Annie?" He had forgotten about the homing instinct.

"No," I said. "Vampires must stay in their home territory. If I attempt to leave Granada Hills, I could die."

"Wow. Is that why Dracula brought dirt from Transylvania to London?"

"There is no Dracula, dude."

Twenty-Nine

Mr. Bach?

I returned to the alleys for fresh air and a little Granada Hills blood. The conversation with Charlie LaGamma did not bode well for our future relationship. It appeared Johnny Depp had pegged him dead right.

A full moon overhead lit up the entire alley off Monogram, and the tall eucalyptus bordering the backyards swayed gently in a steady Santa Susanna breeze.

I loved to peer over the fences and spy on the residents. At the first house a family of five huddled on a couch and watched TV with the lights off. Their blank stares made them resemble cast members from *Night of the Living Dead.*

Two sexy teen girls boldly strutted down the center of the alley. I melted against a fence and didn't move a muscle. They continued their march, weaving and stumbling, raving about an awesome party on Clymer Street. I emerged from the shadows and stalked them silently. I crept up until I was no more than a few inches from their necks. Both girls were giggling and oblivious. I exposed my fangs.

One girl glanced back and got a good look at my face. She screeched and raced down the alley. I was about to chase her down when the other girl stared at me and said, "Mr. Bach?"

Holy crap! I stopped cold and smiled. These girls were two of my seniors from Granada Hills High School. The one who had screamed and bolted stumbled back to us out of breath.

"What the hell, Mr. Bach?" she cried. "You scared the bejeebies out of me."

"Hello, Alex," I said. "Janey."

Alex said, "Mr. Bach, whatta you doing in an alley?" She was slurring her words.

"Might ask you the same thing."

She swayed from the effects of alcohol. "C'mon, tell us."

"I like the solitude," I admitted.

"What's in your mouth, Mr. Bach?" she asked. "I thought I saw fangs."

I laughed. "You did see fangs." I showed her my teeth again. "It's for my new role at the Woodland Hills Theatre. I just got out of rehearsal. We're doing a stage rendition of *Nosferatu, Symphony of Horror*."

"I thought my heart had stopped."

"Sorry, kid. I recognized you both and decided to have some fun."

"Why did you leave Granada?" Alex wailed. "Everyone misses you."

"I've been offered some choice acting roles," I lied. "Theatre has always been my passion."

The sexier one stepped forward and said, "I've always been attracted to you, Mr. Bach."

"You're sweet, Janey."

"I'm eighteen," she said, "and you're no longer my teacher."

My blood said "do her." What was stopping me? There was a good chance neither would remember a thing in the morning. But my heart said "don't you dare."

"Maybe we can have dinner some night," I said.

Just then several high school boys intercepted us. They reeked of sweat and beer.

One of them said, "Wanna Coors, Mr. Bach?"

"Sure, thanks."

Another one said, "I gotta ask a question, Mr. Bach."

"Ask it."

"Why are you wearing make-up?"

They all laughed it up.

"Funny," I said. "First time I've heard that one... today."

"He's in a play at the Woodland Hills Theatre," Janey said.

"Which play? *Return of the Vampire*?"

I exposed my fangs and he jumped back. "Actually..."

They all roared.

Thirty

Betrayal

For reasons I never fully understood nor discovered, Charlie LaGamma was on the brink of financial ruin, and his serious gambling debts were threatening his life. His monetary needs had become a much more serious liability to my survival than my relationship with Annie Mosher.

Charlie and I began to argue.

When I pledged to give him four to five thousand dollars a week, he became enraged and accused me of being miserly and ungrateful. Our relationship began to unravel.

"Make me a vampire, dude," he demanded.

I was stunned. "No way."

"I've watched how you operate," he said. "Vampirism is the answer to all my problems."

"Are you out of your mind? You have no idea what you're asking. The blood addiction is agonizing."

"Make me a vampire, Bach."

I became defiant. "I won't! You're bluffing so I'll continue to do your dirty work."

"Not true, dude," he said. "If you make me a vampire, I won't have to grovel anymore. I won't need you."

"I haven't acquired the skills," I said. "This isn't a Christopher Lee movie."

"You're a liar, Bach. You'd better do what I tell you. I mean it."

"Forget it, dude," I insisted. "We've helped each other and it's been good. I won't abandon you. But no more big scores or vampire talk. It's too dangerous, for both of us."

For a moment he started to break down. "You don't understand, dude."

"What is it?"

"I'm desperate."

"I can provide you with money and protection. I have many vampire friends."

"You're such a fool, Bach. You can't even protect yourself. Annie is playing you. You think I'm your friend, but the truth is I never liked you, not even in Bakersfield. You always acted so superior because you beat me in track and had Annie. Everything was going well until you got cold feet."

"Don't say things like that, dude."

"My luck," he lamented. "I hitched my wagon to a chickenshit vampire."

"I'm your friend."

"What kind of friend would make me beg? The money is easy for you. Why are you being so difficult?

"Let me work on it."

Charlie walked to the front door. He turned back and said, "Get me more money, or else."

"Quit with the tough guy routine, dude."

"I'm not kidding. I'll hurt you."

"You've already hurt me enough tonight."

"I've got another surprise for you, Bach."

I sensed big trouble. Charlie LaGamma knew where I lived and everything else about me, including my relationship with Annie. He flung open his coat and brandished two semiautomatic pistols.

I glared at him menacingly and said, "What the fuck is this?"

"You forced my hand. I want more money."

I moved toward him. He stepped back, but continued to point his guns.

Charlie said, "Careful, dude. These bullets are soaked in mercury."

I took another step forward and suddenly felt nauseous. Charlie was not bluffing. "How do you know about mercury?"

"I had a long talk with Dr. Pares," Charlie said. "Annie told me he was your friend."

I snarled and he shrank toward the door. "If you've hurt Dr. Pares, I'll rip your heart out."

"Relax, Bach," Charlie said. "I didn't do too much damage. Besides, you can't hurt me if I have mercury."

I said, "Leave now and we'll chalk it up as a misunderstanding. We can still be friends."

"I don't want to be your friend."

"You disappoint me, dude."

"Do as I say," he said. "Make me a vampire or get me loads of cash. Otherwise, I'll destroy you."

"Then do it now," I hissed. "I don't care. I barely made ten weeks."

Charlie said, "It's not that easy, dude. I have other plans."

"I won't help you."

"You better start thinking about Annie. If anything happens to me or I don't get what I want, I've instructed several associates to open a safe deposit box that contains a contract and promissory note for ten thousand dollars to any group or individual who will murder your girlfriend. She lives in Chatsworth and you can't protect her outside of Granada Hills."

"If you kill Annie you'll get nothing."

"Same as I'm getting now."

"Big scores are too reckless. We'll get caught."

Charlie sneered. "Maybe you can hook me up with a vampire who has some balls."

"Don't talk like that."

Charlie flashed an ordinary kitchen knife that had been dipped in mercury and I nearly fell on my ass. He said, "I'll kill Annie and Dr. Pares, and then I'll kill you."

I said, "I'll bring a wad a cash to El Presidente tomorrow night."

"Now you're talking, dude," Charlie said.

I remembered he had told me about his safe deposit box in North Hollywood. I had to trick him into revealing the location of his bank. I wrote on a piece of paper.

"Here's the name and address of a vampire in Granada Hills who will help you with money if anything should happen to me. Keep it in a safe place. This should prove my sincerity."

Charlie slipped the piece of paper into his wallet. "You better bring a load of jack to El Presidente."

After he left I called Dr. Pares twice but there was no answer.

Thirty-One

Path to Destruction

After Charlie LaGamma left my apartment, I returned to the alleys for a little Granada Hills blood. An attractive middle-aged soccer mom was in the alley searching for her cat. She appeared quite fetching as she bent over to look under a car. I motioned for the cat to stay against the tire.

As I approached her, a powerful hand drew me back. It was the slender vampire girl.

She asked, "What were you planning? Sex on the hood of the car?"

I grinned. "I'm not that innovative. I'm only ten weeks old."

"You may not live to be ten weeks and a day."

"Why do you say that?"

"I've been following you."

I shrugged. "So what?"

"Do you really love the blonde girl?"

"I think I do."

"This will end badly, Bach," she said. "Why don't you stay with me?"

She was serious. "I didn't think you cared."

"I'm not jealous, if that's what you think, but you should stay with your own kind."

"You insisted we couldn't have a relationship."

Her long black hair covered one eye. "I didn't want to make it too easy."

I had to laugh. Johnny Depp was correct about females. I said, "You don't live in West Hollywood with a coven of vampires, do you?"

She appeared startled. "How do you know that?"

"Vampires can't leave their home turf," I said. "You live in Granada Hills."

"I do live in Granada Hills," she admitted, "but you're wrong about not being able to leave the home turf."

"Am I?"

"The homing instinct is powerful. You've sensed the boundaries. However, although it's not pleasant, you can leave for short periods of time. Bram Stoker wrote that Dracula carried dirt from his Transylvania homeland in order to adjust to London. But you must practice before you try it."

"I don't have time for practice. I'm leaving tomorrow."

She grinned. "Then you're going to have to suck it up."

"Funny," I said. "I never heard that one. Is it safe?"

"It's never safe. We are vampires."

"Can I make it?"

"Yes, but it'll be painful. I've visited West Hollywood many times. It gets easier with practice."

"Will you help me?"

"I can follow and pull you out if there's a problem."

"I'm going to Charlie's townhouse in North Hollywood."

"That's not the solution, Bach. I know what you should do."

"What's that?"

"Forget Charlie and the blonde and move to a different apartment. You can stay with me for a while."

I shook my head. "I can't. There's something I gotta do."

She looked dejected. "Something wicked is coming your way."

Thirty-Two

North Hollywood

At 7:30 a.m. I drove my black Mustang to North Hollywood and parked outside of Charlie LaGamma's townhouse. The sun had just risen. I wore a silver long-sleeved Under Armour shirt, UCLA Bruins hat, sunglasses and a pair of thin Calvin Klein touring gloves. For luck I rubbed some dirt from Granada Hills on my arms. As soon as I had crossed into Mission Hills my insides felt like they might implode. In North Hollywood, I thought I was going to die. In the rearview mirror I could clearly see the slender vampire girl parked in a silver Jeep Wrangler. She was also wearing sunglasses, long-sleeves and a hat.

At about 8:45 a.m., Charlie LaGamma emerged from the courtyard and drove off in his BMW. I was counting on him to go to his bank and drop off the slip of paper with the fake vampire name and address. I had chosen the name Robert Quarry, an obscure actor who had starred in the

1970s *Count Yorga* films. I doubted Charlie would appreciate my humor.

During the time I waited for Charlie, I grew increasingly sick and agitated. It was a bad move to leave Granada Hills, but I saw no other alternative. Charlie would not expect it. My sickness forced me to vomit in my car. I had debunked so many dopey myths about vampires, it seemed only fair I would fall victim to a new twist. I wondered if Bram Stoker really was a vampire. Maybe I should have filled my backseat with Granada Hills dirt.

Damn it, Charlie parked in front of his office. Now what? But when he hopped out of his car, he crossed the street and entered a Bank of America. He was inside for maybe fifteen minutes. After he left, I climbed out of my car and walked into the bank.

"May I help you, sir?" a clerk at the safe deposit gate asked.

"No, thank you," I said, grabbing him by the neck and snatching his keys. I put him down softly, careful not to let his head strike the tile floor, and unlocked the cage door. It was simple to locate Charlie's box with my sense of smell. I had rubbed the note with my fingers. Since I was made in

Granada Hills, my skin smelled like eucalyptus. It took a nanosecond to open the lock and remove the manila envelope that contained all the information that could destroy Dr. Pares and Annie Mosher.

I helped the clerk to his feet. "Are you okay?"

"What happened?"

I said, "You took a nasty spill. I think you fainted."

"I don't remember."

"Lucky you didn't hit your head."

He rubbed his eyes. "Yeah, I guess."

I drove along Devonshire and passed a sign with a Highlander playing a bagpipe that read, "Welcome to Granada Hills, Home of the Fighting Scots." I felt better instantly. The slender vampire girl waved and turned her silver Jeep Wrangler onto Balboa. I drove directly to my apartment with plans to recuperate and put on my game face.

Thirty-Three

Killer

Early in the evening I sat in the parking lot at El Presidente and waited. The customary *fiesta loca* was raging on the covered patio.

Charlie LaGamma arrived at 9:00 p.m. He walked up to the passenger side, pulled a semiautomatic loaded with mercury soaked bullets, and pointed it at my face.

I snarled and bared my fangs. "Put the gun on top of the car," I hissed. "I mean it, Charlie. I won't give you any money if you're pointing a gun at me."

Charlie chuckled. "Mercury puts you in a foul mood, dude." He placed the gun on the roof of the car and slid into my passenger seat.

"Thank you," I said.

"You need to behave, dude." He brandished a silver ice pick that had been dipped in mercury. "Amazing what you can buy at Wal-Mart."

"I promised you a steady stream of cash," I said. "Stop this nonsense with the mercury."

"Or what?"

I glanced out the window. "Or I'll kill you, dude."

Charlie puffed with bravado. "Even if you did kill me, which is unlikely, have you forgotten about what's in my safe deposit box in North Hollywood? If I die, Dr. Pares and Annie will die within a week. If my associates don't kill you tonight, all the information needed to destroy you is also in the box. Now stop screwing around and give me the cash."

I opened my leather coat. "Here you go, dude," I said, flopping the manila envelope from the safe deposit box onto his lap. At first he didn't comprehend, then he realized what I had done and stared at me.

"You're dead, Bach."

I wagged my finger at him. "If you reach for the gun, I'll break your fingers."

He lunged at me with the ice pick, but I flicked it out the window and grabbed his throat. My thumb got nicked and started to bleed.

Charlie quickly realized he had blundered.

"Bach," he gasped, "please stop. I can still help you. I told you Annie is playing you, but I didn't mention she has a boyfriend who's in on it. He's a dangerous son of a bitch."

"It's over, dude," I said icily.

"Listen to me, Bach. They've hatched a scheme to control you. I was going to warn you as soon as you came up with the money. Don't trust those big green eyes." I squeezed with force. "Bach," he cried. "Go Roadrunners."

Blood streamed from his mouth. "Sorry, Charlie," I said, and eased him back against the headrest.

I climbed out of the car and carried him to a bench along the patio wall. Several patrons stared at me. I winked at them and said, "Best margaritas in the Valley." They roared with laughter.

I wrapped my thumb with duct tape and cursed under my breath. I had just killed my best friend and was going directly to hell.

Thirty-Four

Evil

Books and movies portray vampires as evil. They can also be suave, humorous and sexy, but they are still monsters and killers. They are evil.

I'm a vampire. I don't feel evil and, in fact, I'm not even sure what constitutes evil. I take blood, but that is my nature. Is a mountain lion that takes blood for his evening meal evil? Until tonight I had never killed.

I'm a seducer and addict. I'm also friendly, considerate and merciful. I care about people and the world, and have a capacity for love. I also have a sense of loyalty and justice.

I'm a vampire.

I don't know if Charlie LaGamma was evil, but he certainly wasn't very good. He was greedy. He not only exploited our friendship, he was willing to murder Dr. Pares and Annie Mosher over money. Most people are not evil. I don't believe in the concept of Original Sin. The idea of sin is gibberish spouted by organized religion.

Satan does not exist. All people have a choice between good and evil; it is the nature of existence. The only evil in the world is the heart of darkness.

I killed Charlie LaGamma because he threatened to kill my friends and me. Is that not self-defense? Is not self-defense justifiable homicide? Good people kill in wars.

Do people who are evil think they are good? Do people who are good wonder if they are evil? I wrapped more duct tape around my thumb.

I felt lonely and very depressed.

Thirty-Five

Annie Makes Her Play

The following evening I rendezvoused with Annie Mosher at the Odyssey Restaurant. As we strolled across the parking lot I scanned the perimeter for the slender vampire girl, but was fairly certain she wouldn't reveal herself. Did she really care or was she simply curious about my fate? I wondered. If Annie weren't in the picture would I be in love with the vampire girl?

It was a seductive November evening and the view from the Odyssey was delectable. Annie led me to the bar for an Irish whiskey over ice. She was dressed to kill, in a slinky dark green dress. Most of the male patrons stared at her rather than the wicked view of the Valley.

"I was afraid you weren't coming," she said. When I touched her arm she was trembling. "I thought I had lost you."

I shook my head. "Why would you think that?"

"I treated you so badly in Bakersfield. I'm still frightened that you hate me."

I said, "I'm happy now. Granada Hills is not Bakersfield."

"I was absolutely wretched," she continued, "and I didn't even feel bad about it at the time."

"Bakersfield is a hundred years ago," I said, and grinned. "Not much more about that needs to be said."

Her laugh was infectious. "I suppose I'll have to force myself to be nice to Charlie LaGamma."

"What for?"

"He's responsible for getting us back together."

I took hold of her hand. "There's a slight problem with Charlie LaGamma."

She looked up at me. "What did he tell you?"

I finished my drink. "That wasn't what I meant, but he did say you had a boyfriend."

She flashed her trademark wounded expression. "He told you about my boyfriend?"

"Yep."

"I had a boyfriend when Charlie called me about you," she said. "I broke it off after our first date."

"Charlie implied the contrary."

"He was lying."

"Why would he lie?"

"He's only concerned about money," she said. "He threatened to blackmail me over the boyfriend. What did you do to your finger?"

I shrugged. "What do you really want, Annie?"

She batted her huge green eyes. "Let's eat dinner first."

A pretty hostess led us to an outdoor table where the Valley lights were blinking at our feet. The fire in the pit kicked up a bright flame. For a change the evening was lucid and the lights in the North Hollywood hills twinkled.

"Order for me, Bach," Annie cooed.

I selected stuffed sea bass with a bottle of Simi chardonnay.

"I'm going to make it work this time," she said. "I want you to teach me how to satisfy a vampire."

"I'm only eleven weeks old. We'll learn together."

"Do you forgive me for Bakersfield?"

"Annie, please."

"I need to know, Bach. Don't play games."

"You hurt me badly," I admitted, "but I forgive you."

"I'm going to make you so happy," she said in her husky Lauren Bacall voice.

I eyed the freckles on her chest. She reminded me of a sexy song by the rock band Nickelback. The short dress exposed her long legs with blonde down on the inner thighs. A girl like Annie could ignite wars.

"Let's go to my apartment," I said. "I need a little Granada Hills blood."

We made it no further than the black Mustang. I pushed Annie's seat back so she could be nearly vertical. The top of her dress was down and the bottom up. After our first round, Annie made her play.

"Make me a vampire, Bach." It was exactly what Johnny Depp had predicted. "We can live together and do this every night."

I shook my head. "It would be no good. Vampires don't stay with each other."

"We can change the rules."

I was suspicious. I argued against the proposition, but she wore me down.

"I won't leave you, Bach," she said, sitting on my lap.

I said, "It's too dangerous. Something could go wrong. Let's wait until I gain more experience."

"Charlie claimed you turned the doctor's wife."

Damn him, I thought. Then, I remembered he was dead.

"She almost died," I lied.

"I'm not afraid."

Once more I glanced at her freckled chest. "I killed Charlie last night. He threatened to kill you and the doctor."

Her expression never changed. "Good for you."

"He was my best friend."

"Some best friend, Bach. He tried to coerce me into having sex with him."

"If I make you a vampire, you'll leave me."

"No," she cried. "I'll treat you well."

She climbed off my lap and pushed down her dress. "Do it, Bach. Do me now."

It was useless to refuse. I explained how she would feel dangerously weak, but when she drank my blood the change would occur quickly. She listened and nodded excitedly.

I said, "There'll be a moment when both of us are vulnerable. It will be crucial not to panic or attract attention."

"I trust you," she said.

"You'll recover first. Beware. You'll experience an alarming pain from your addiction, and blood will be your new drug of necessity. Your thirst will be overwhelming. Do not—I repeat—do not take down a mark at the restaurant or in its parking lot. It could create a dangerous situation."

"What should I do?"

"Wait for me," I said, "if you can stand it."

"What if I can't?"

I pointed to the edge of the lot. "Do you see the dirt path?"

"Yes."

"Follow the dirt path down the hill to the Granada Inn on the corner of Rinaldi and the 405. Go to room number sixteen. A group of day laborers rent the room. Take your blood, but do not kill anyone. We are not killers. You will sense the moment when you should stop. After the mark weakens, set him down making certain his head does not strike the floor.

Wait for me in the room. As soon as I recover I'll pick you up in the Mustang."

"I'll do everything you say," she said. She was actually beginning to moan. I bit the back of her shoulder. She stiffened but offered no resistance. She went limp in my arms.

"Steady, girl," I whispered. "Here comes the tricky part."

Her eyes glazed over. I cut my wrist and pressed it to her lips. At first she only licked as the blood streamed down her cheek. Once she got a good taste, however, she seized my arm and drank heartily. She fell back into the passenger seat and began to snarl.

"Prepare for the thirst," I reminded her. "It will come at any moment."

I felt like crap, much worse than after Rosamund Pares. I could barely lift my head or arms. Annie was like a tigress. When she looked at me, her green eyes shimmered. Her breath on my face smelled like Granada Hills sage.

She leaned in closer and said, "I need more blood, Bach."

I felt a twinge of recovery. "Go to room number sixteen and take what you need. Do not kill them or leave the room."

Her fangs were white and perfectly shaped. "What happens if I kill?"

"Don't do it. You'll become addicted to the jolt and turn into a murderer."

She climbed out of the car. "I'm going now, Bach."

"I'll pick you up at the room."

From the thick brush along the parking lot a raspy voice said, "You ain't picking up anyone, Sport." A tall muscular man with a ponytail approached the car on the driver's side and flashed a large .357 revolver. I sensed mercury.

I attempted to swat the gun out of his hand, but Annie reached back into the car and caught my arm. Then she leaned out of the way. The gun blast was deafening. The bullet punched me in the chest and knocked me across the passenger seat and onto the pavement. I hit my head and saw a lightning bolt.

The man with the ponytail said, "That looked like it really hurt."

From the ground, I said, "The boyfriend, I presume."

"Things just aren't going your way tonight, Sport," he said.

I tried to bluff. "You can't hurt me with that thing, dude."

He walked around the car and said, "I soaked the bullets with mercury."

I glanced at Annie. The extent of her betrayal was stunning. "You told him about mercury? That was dumb. He can use it against you."

"I'm going to shoot you in both kneecaps just for fun."

"Kosmo," Annie snapped. "Stop it."

"Shut up, girl," he replied.

"Kosmo?" I said. "I feel like I'm in an episode of *Seinfeld*."

"You've been played, Sport," Kosmo said. "You're a two-time sucker."

"Don't taunt him," Annie demanded.

"It doesn't matter, Annie," I said. "I was warned to stay away, but I didn't care. I wanted my girlfriend back."

"You need a tissue, Sport?" Kosmo asked. He raised the gun.

"He's a threat to you, Annie," I hissed. "He knows how to destroy you."

Kosmo laughed.

Summoning every ounce of strength, I performed a roundhouse kick from the ground aimed at Kosmo's leg, and cut him down before he could shoot again. The gun clattered to the pavement. A loud snap was proof positive I had broken an ankle or shin. Kosmo howled with pain.

Annie was crazed with thirst. I said, "There's no time to make it to the Granada Inn, Annie. Succumb to the thirst."

"What can I do?" she cried.

"Take Kosmo," I said. "Take him down. I'm offering him to you on a platter."

Kosmo attempted to stand up. "Don't listen to him, Annie," he screamed. "Go to the Granada Inn."

Blood flowed from my wound. The bullet may have nicked a lung. I had to get back to my apartment.

"Don't wait any longer, Annie," I said. "Take your drug."

I saw in her eyes I had won. So did Kosmo. She turned and pounced on him. She did it so quickly he barely had time to whimper.

"Take as much as you need," I said, crawling over the console into the driver's seat. I knew she was going to kill him.

Popping the clutch, I punched the gas pedal and roared across the parking lot and down the hill in reverse. The Mustang fishtailed onto Rinaldi. I pressed Annie's panties over the wound to my chest and braced my back against the seat. That seemed to stem the flow of blood.

Careening onto Woodly, I zipped past John F. Kennedy High School and conjured up a vision of our President and the bloodbath in Dallas. Passing La Rosa Liquors and the Burrito Factory, I was amazed I was still alive. After a quick right onto Chatsworth, I uncorked the V-8 and laid rubber in each gear. I ran red lights at Hayvenhurst and Balboa.

At Louise, I pulled into the back alley and parked in my spot.

Thirty-Six

Family

I closed my journal and struggled to remain conscious. Because of the mercury, my wounds would never stop bleeding or heal. Blood continued to drip on the wood floor, and the dark pool grew larger and larger.

Stand up, I commanded. Drive to Holy Cross Hospital and Dr. Pares. But it was no use. I shouldn't have come home to write my story.

Suddenly, the front door smashed off its hinges and a blur raced across my living room. It was the slender vampire girl. She slung me over her shoulder.

I said, "I didn't make twelve weeks."

"We're taking you to Dr.Pares," she said. "He's expecting you."

"We?"

She motioned with her head toward the front door. Rosamund Pares stood guard at the railing.

Rosamund said, "My husband can save you, Bach."

"It's too late."

"Don't say that," the slender vampire girl said. "We're here now."

I looked into her beautiful black eyes. "I don't even know your name."

She smiled. "My name is Sophie."

I nodded. "Let's take my black Mustang, Sophie."

She said, "No, he wants to drive."

I looked. Parked at the curb, with its engine revving, was a gorgeous shiny red Camaro. Johnny Depp was clutching the steering wheel.

"Hold on, kid," he said.

This was my finest moment as a vampire. I finally had a real family.

Acknowledgments

I wish to thank Hal Zina Bennett for not forgetting about me.

Thank you to my editor and brother-in-arms Daniel Barth.

Thanks to Carl Brush for reading and making suggestions.

Special thanks to Christopher Lee. Dude, you are the finest vampire of them all.

About the Author

G. Kent lives in the wilds of the Ocala National Forest in North Florida. He was born and raised in Los Angeles. He is also the author of *Bandits on the Rim* (Tenacity Press, 2012) and *Grinners* (Bandit Press, 2014). For more information, contact kentib@earthlink.net.

Made in the USA
San Bernardino, CA
31 December 2016